Praise for *The Terr*

'Gripping dystopia with a keen political e
Imogen Russell Williams, *Metro*

'A pacy dystopian fantasy thriller'
Martin Chilton, *The Telegraph*, **best YA books of 2015**

'This is a truly exceptional novel, exciting, gripping and intense, with relatable protagonists whose agonies become the reader's own. It deals with complex moral dilemmas regarding loyalty, self-preservation and family, forcing the reader to answer the uncomfortable question: who deserves to live when spaces are limited? This is the first of a trilogy and the final cliff-hanger will leave you clamouring for more.'

Book Trust

'Truly heart-wrenching! Govett raises issues about our education system, the environment and decisions governments around the world are making. I'd go so far as to call this the 1984 of our time and recommend this as a great read, with a fantastic political context.'

The Guardian children's books site

'Govett has created a powerful and shocking novel that makes the reader wonder how societies would deal with the environmental consequences of climate change and if there could ever be any 'right' course of action ... an excellent, thought-provoking book.'

Children's Books Ireland

'...an enjoyable, fast-paced read, and raises some interesting questions about how you would behave in difficult situations, as well as being a clear indictment of the UK education system...'

Books for Keeps

'The Territory is a terrific book. It simply is.'

Bookwitch

'I loved every second of this book; it was phenomenal.'

Yourbestbookpal

Sarah Govett, 37, read law at Trinity College, Oxford. After qualifying as a solicitor, she set up her own tutoring agency. Her first book, *The Territory* was shortisted for the Times/Chicken House fiction competition and published by Firefly in 2015 to considerable acclaim.

She has two young children and lives in London.

THE TERRITORY, ESCAPE

First published in 2016
by Firefly Press
25 Gabalfa Road, Llandaff North, Cardiff, CF14 2JJ
www.fireflypress.co.uk

A CIP catalogue record of this book is available from the British Library.

Print ISBN 978-1-910080-46-7
epub ISBN 978-1-910080-47-4

This book has been published with the support of the Welsh Books Council.

Typeset by: Elaine Sharples

Printed by Pulsio SARL

THE
TERRITORY,
ESCAPE

SARAH GOVETT

Firefly

For Earl

For the first few days I couldn't stop looking at my hands. Well, my right hand to be exact. The hand Raf had squeezed when we'd promised to get Jack back. I'd wanted his fingers to have branded mine, like a tattoo or something, but they hadn't. They'd just left faint bruises that faded and even when I kept pinching the same patches at night like some kind of weird OCD ritual they wouldn't come back. Turns out it's pretty hard to bruise yourself. Others though…

Memories fade too. Maybe it's the brain's way of protecting yourself. All you're left with is snapshots.

FLASH

Jack being dragged off with the others in his cage to become Fish. He was the only one not crying. Like he was resigned to it and that was somehow worse. He even smiled at me – this slow calm smile – cheeks bunching freckles – as if he was trying to cheer me up. Like I was the one who'd been hurt. He couldn't stop protecting me even at the end.

FLASH

Sitting in silence on the bus on the way back home. Not that it felt like proper home anymore. Not without Jack. A little part of him, a little part of us, was in everything I did and everywhere I went and that made his not being there even more real.

FLASH

Mum and Dad's reaction when I told them. Dad was angry. The sort of angry that tenses every muscle in your body and even changes your build, your height.

'Bastards,' he hissed. Dad's never angry and he NEVER says bastards. Mum wasn't angry. She wasn't even doing her super straight back thing. She was scared and couldn't keep her eyes off me, scanning my face – like she was trying to do some sort of retinal lie-detector. 'You're not thinking of doing anything stupid are you, Noa?' she asked eventually. I shook my head. I didn't want to lie to her and not saying the words seemed to make it less of a lie.

But I couldn't lie to myself. It was my fault that Jack had failed and been shipped off to the Wetlands. I knew it, felt it, with every cell of my body. Every time I looked in the mirror, an executioner's face stared back at me. He'd got the pass mark. He'd be here with us now, if only he hadn't run. If only he'd hadn't been standing there in the corridor. If only I hadn't said I didn't want him. I was drowning in a sea of 'if onlys'. I had to make it right.

Raf and I had originally agreed to wait for two weeks before going after Jack. We reckoned it'd give us time to plan, get supplies, spend some time with our families – well, in Raf's case, his mum. His horrific dad worked such long hours it would be easy enough to avoid him. This meant going through the motions of 'normal' post-TAA, which basically meant filling in forms for Further Education Schools. It also usually meant going to celebration parties.

The parties we could avoid. Very few other Norms had passed and we didn't feel like hanging out with the Childes. I couldn't be around them, couldn't see the Nodes at the back of their necks without picturing them uploading, shaking gently as information shot from their terminals into their brains. Success for them had been guaranteed. Smugness seemed pretty much guaranteed too. I tried not to hate them. Tried to remember that their personalities were being warped by whatever poisonous thoughts the Ministry was hiding in the uploads. Tried to remember that if Raf hadn't made the decision not to upload, he would've been exactly like them – another Norm-hating freakoid.

The FES forms couldn't be escaped as easily though. Mum had gone on and on at me to apply as students were supposed to do this within a week of passing, as if she was looking for any sign that I wasn't committing to life here. To life after Jack.

'Noa-bean, you just have to pick a school and choose three subjects. Don't think any further than that. One step at a time.'

Raf and I put the same school and the same subject combination: Biology, Chemistry and Physics. We could have chosen Maths or History (or rather lies about The Territory according to the Ministry), but neither appealed. I'd really wanted to do English but that wasn't an option at any of the 'good' schools. No surprise there.

'A scientist like your mum,' Dad said proudly.

I don't know what expression I pulled, I wasn't trying to make a point or anything, at least not consciously, but it was enough to make Dad wince. Mum wasn't there. Scientists in Mum's department were *working late* at the moment. Lots of work now after the exams – those kids who'd failed the TAA and had been abandoned by their parents weren't going to experiment on themselves. No, someone had to inject them with hideous viruses and then muck about with finding cures.

Mum's not sleeping well at the moment. She's got dark hollows under her eyes and new creases in her forehead. We don't talk about it. There's nothing to say. I understand it now. The choice she made. That she had to make. The only time she came close to mentioning it was one night when she thought I was asleep. She sat at the end of my bed and hugged my old teddy, Winston, who still sits there. Lame I know, but if you've given something a name and talked to it most of your life, it seems somehow wrong, kind of cruel, to then go and shut it up in a box somewhere.

'This'll be the last year, Winston. The last year,' Mum murmured into his mangy fur and the bed shook a bit so she was probably crying.

Dad said he'd check over my FES form before I sent it in – cast his legal eagle eye over it in case I'd malced something up. He was smiling all the way through the first couple of paragraphs. I'd clearly managed to format and spell everything right. Noa Blake – not a total denser. Then he got to the 'Choice of College' section and his face visibly drooped. He called Mum over with one of their psychic gazes. This one must have been a distress signal.

'Did you know Noa's applying to Greenhaven?'

Mum didn't and her face drooped too – like they were both plants in a dried-up flowerbed. She clearly wasn't a fan of me going to a boarding school in the Third City either.

'I need some distance. I see him … everywhere.'

They nodded. They got it and didn't need to ask who *he* was. And Greenhaven was one of the 'best' schools.

I think what hurt Mum and Dad more was that Raf and I'd applied for the 'Early Start Programme' (for losers who wanted to study pre-term courses for a month before normal lessons started.)

Mum had difficulty getting the words out. 'Your dad and me had thought we could spend some time together. All together. As a family. Now that it's over.' Her face was an abstract canvas of panic. 'If it's something we've done… *I've* done, we can change things. They might let me sever my contract before the year's up.'

But that wasn't an option. We all knew that. No one left a Ministry funded position mid-year. Mum'd be under suspicion. On a list.

'It's not that, Mum. It's … I need to unscramble my head. And I can't do it here.'

It was true even if it wasn't the exact truth behind what we were doing. Raf and I had decided it'd be easier to leave this way. To tell our parents we'd applied for the Early Start Programme when we'd actually applied to start at the normal time in August. This meant we'd have a month before anyone official would know we were AWOL. Mum and Dad wouldn't know either. Visits weren't allowed until half-term and there weren't any shared phones or anything. By the time you're at an FES, 'everyone's family' say the ads. Cue massive picture of smug, smiling teenager who looks likes he's had extra teeth crammed into his mouth. But what they're basically saying is that the Ministry's going to take over the role of parent from now on thank you very much. Step up the indoctrination a notch.

The Early Start Programme began on 7 July. This meant we'd be leaving four weeks after the TAA instead of two, but that was still OK we told ourselves. It meant we'd be more ready. Better able to help Jack when we got there. And we'd have a chance at getting back before we were missed, which was crucial if we wanted to protect our families from investigation. Parents of defectors weren't treated so well. How exactly we were going to do that, get back, with Jack miraculously concealed, hadn't come to us yet. But we didn't have time to wait until a plan was formed. We had to just hope it did.

The acceptance from Greenhaven came three days later and then it was like we were on some conveyor belt. Uniforms and initial reading arrived. We were sent our timetable, allocated a dorm. Raf and me spent every minute we could together – at one or other of our houses – never in public – and kept on going through the motions. Before we knew it we were even reading some of the material, first to distract ourselves and then because it was actually kind of interesting.

Like the stuff on genetic engineering. It's amazing what scientists can do, what people are working on. Splicing a gene from a species of seaweed into a potato plant to produce salt tolerant varieties; adapting a species of Mucor so that it produces Vitamins A and C to make it more nutritious.

I was all, 'This is incredible, we could engineer anything – Mucor that actually tastes good.'

'Don't set your sights so low,' Raf replied, his eyes sparkling stones. 'We could bring back pets. Think about it. If they could work out how to engineer some that photosynthesise… Come on – you've got to admit it – green dogs would be awesome.'

I started to crack up then stopped mid-laugh. It felt wrong. The action. The movement of my ribcage. The smile plastered across my face. And 'dogs' brought back too many memories. Memories of Rex. Me, Jack and Rex. Jack's drawing of a dog, and of his dad. His real dad, who'd joined the Opposition and been 'eliminated'. The rest of my laugh coagulated in my throat.

Raf, almost as if reading my mind, whispered, 'Sorry, Noa. I know things are hard. Horribly hard at the moment. But it's OK to laugh. Don't see it as a betrayal. See it as a way of fighting back.'

I nodded, but the laughter didn't return.

We read on and there was this chapter all about 'exercising caution'. About how scientists had tried to eliminate malaria entirely thirty-five years ago by engineering and breeding a larger species of mosquito that couldn't carry the malarial plasmodium. This larger mosquito was then supposed to outcompete the malarial mosquitoes thereby depriving the plasmodium of a host and destroying the disease in the process. It didn't work. The plasmodium evolved. It could use the bigger mosquito after all. Malaria went massive.

'No wonder they didn't teach us this stuff earlier,' I said slowly, anger growing. 'Imagine knowing you were going to fail and be a Fish and be sent to die from something that THEY made much worse than it should have been.'

'They messed with mosquitoes long before the Ministry's time,' Raf countered.

'I know. But it's the same, don't you see? It's all the same. People playing God.'

This morning I was curled into Raf's shoulder, comforted by the warmth of his body and the smell of the dip of skin by his collarbone where sweat collects when he's hot or nervous. Even his sweat smells nice – musky and smoky. Well it smells nice there anyway – once he kicked off his trainers to sit on the floor and his socks or trainers, whichever, really stank. Maybe feet produce a different type of sweat. But back to his collarbone – lying there I felt safe. For the first time in a long time. It was like I was drugged or something. I was so used to feeling super stressed that feeling relaxed was weird. Like my body had lost half its bones and a plastic insert had been removed from my jaw.

Raf was reading *The Biology of Plants*. 'In case any of it helped us survive in the Wetlands.' He'd read a page then summarise it for me. Partly because I was feeling lazy and partly because it meant I'd get to watch him read. See the way his forehead crinkled when he got to a difficult bit and his mouth twitched when he got to something pretentious or amusing. Pretentious I guess. Biology, particularly the biology of plants, isn't exactly hilarious. Then he'd finish and gaze blue and green down at me and it was like I was watching Earth from space. And I relearnt how to laugh. The guilt didn't go exactly, but it sort of lost its density – became a thin veil of mist instead of a thick layer of fog. We laughed about the most stupid things. Apparently the mole above my belly button is the shape of a moonwort fern spore, which might not sound funny, but was, massively so. Then Raf pretended he had super powers by taking off his jumper and rubbing it on my arm to make all the hairs stand on end, wiggling his fingers at the same time to look like he was somehow magnetising the hairs up or something. I hope they're an acceptable level of hairy. I'd never really looked at them that closely before, but Raf didn't look grimmed out or anything.

This evening at dinner I also actually chatted properly with Mum and Dad. And every now and then they'd just grin, grin like little kids, just because they were so pleased I'd made it and their girl had finally come home.

And part of me, God I hate to admit it, but part of me, wanted this to be it. Our life. Not pretending. Studying and living with Raf, seeing Mum and Dad in the holidays. In the Third City no one would know our past – Raf wouldn't have to pretend he hated me. Norms who'd passed were treated OK. I wouldn't get a top job but I could have a life. A real life.

Dad interrupted my thoughts. 'When do you leave, baby?'

'The seventh,' I replied. And it was only when I lay down in bed that I realised quite how involved I'd become in my cover-story. Like a spy in too deep. In my head I wasn't leaving for the Wetlands on the seventh, I was leaving to study, I was leaving for Greenhaven.

A piece of yellow paper changed everything.

I knew something was wrong as soon as I walked through the door. Mum had red eyes and was doing her super-straight-back thing. Seeing me looking at her, she pointed at the paper, struggling to get the words out.

'It's a forced sale notice,' she explained. 'For Aunty Vicki's house… A courtesy from the Ministry.' She semi-spat the last words.

The forced sale in itself wasn't odd – houses of criminals, dissidents, parents of kids who'd run away before the TAA were all automatically repossessed by the Ministry and sold, the money going straight into the Ministry coffers. The thing was, normally other family members weren't even informed. The notice was just tacked to the outside of the property before the clearance team stripped it out. They wouldn't have rushed to get round to Aunty Vicki's house as they always focused on the most valuable first. A run-down place right by the Fence was hardly prime real estate.

Then Mum properly broke down. 'They told me Noa, the Ministry officials who came here and gave me THIS,' her hands gave a violent tremor. 'They told me they were informing me because I hadn't helped her. Because I hadn't helped my own SISTER.'

I rushed over to comfort her. 'You can't feel guilty, Mum. You did it for us. For me. To keep us all safe. You had no choice.'

'No Noa, you don't understand [gut wrenching sob]. They knew.'

I looked blank. I didn't get it. 'But how … how could they know?'

Deep breath.

'Aunty Vicki told them.'

I sat/collapsed down.

'What…?' tears were streaming down my face before I'd even registered it in my brain. They'd caught them. We hadn't helped them and now they'd been caught.

No answer.

'So they're Fish now. Oh God, Oh God.' I couldn't stop shaking.

'Ella is.' Three deep breaths. 'Aunty Vicki *didn't survive questioning*. The evil, evil BASTARDS.' Mum shouted this last bit and my eyes fled to the door. Please, please don't let anyone be listening. I think Mum's outburst even shocked her, so she pulled herself together a bit and lowered her voice. 'They're letting me get any belongings I want from her house, because I've proved myself to be a "loyal citizen". And look…' Mum uncurled a shaking fist '…they've even given me a medal.'

And there it sat in the palm of her hand. A flat silver disc with the symbol of the Territory embossed in it.

Apparently gold was reserved for families that went one step further and actually called in to inform on their fleeing relatives.

Mum and I got to Aunty Vicki's house just before 9am. We'd got up when it was still dark and driven through the dawn. There was something therapeutic about seeing the world come alive.

I know it was just in my head but the house seemed different, even from a distance – emptier and smaller too.

Mum pushed open the door – Auntie Vicki never locked it, I don't even know if she had a key – and we entered. I was practically glued to Mum's side the whole time as I knew she couldn't face doing this alone.

Everything was as they'd left it – from the pans upside down on the draining rack to the open book propped up on the table. The house even still smelt of them. Not like a stench or anything, but in the way that other people's houses always smell a certain way and only yours smells normal. Apart from a thin layer of dust, you'd imagine Aunty Vicki and Ella were just out back, about to come in and get on with their lives. I guess that's what they wanted everyone to think. In case anyone came snooping round. So no one would report them gone immediately.

Mum had brought a box and started putting stuff in – the photo from the mantelpiece of them as girls, a photo album of Ella growing up, any left-over dried food from the cupboard. Mum looked guiltily at me when she was packing up the food, but with rations and everything it was the right thing to do – anyone would have done it, right? It'd be dense not to.

When the boxes were full, Mum spent hours just drifting. Taking remaining clothes out of drawers and holding them, looking at the failing vegetables in the garden that Aunty Vicki could never get to grow right because of the salt. Her mouth would move every now and then but she wouldn't be speaking to me. She was talking to herself – or maybe to Aunty Vicki. In any event, she was away somewhere intensely private in her head and it seemed rude to ask anything about it.

To give her space, I went to sit in Ella's room and, without really thinking about it, started going through the same sort of ritual. Ella's favourite skirt was draped over the back of the chair – black, short and puffball. I guess not that suitable for trekking cross-country. Fighting back the tears, I sat at her desk, running my hand over the rough wood. The desk was empty apart from a clear pencil case with pen, pencil, protractor, compass, rubber – all ready for the exams she never sat.

We were spending the night there, Mum and me, and as the light started to fade I fetched our sleeping bags in from the car. It didn't seem right to sleep in their beds. They seemed sacred somehow – like a memorial. Or a tomb.

Mum found a bottle of whiskey amongst Aunty Vicki's food supplies and solemnly poured us each an inch. We clinked glasses. 'To Vicki – may she rest in peace. To Ella – God be with her.' Mum doesn't believe in God. Not unless everything is so, so awful that nothing she does believe in can help. Mum downed her glass in one and quickly poured herself another while I nearly choked on my first and only sip. Whiskey's rank.

Mum fell asleep quite quickly, but it clearly wasn't peaceful. She'd twist and her face would contort and once this short scream and the word 'Sorry' just burst out.

I couldn't sleep. Didn't have the help of the whiskey, I guess. I don't think my mind could have switched off anyway. All I kept thinking about was Jack. How I'd nearly forgotten my promise to him already. How instead I'd wanted to make a fake lie of a life in the Territory – a place that sent kids to die and tortured people who tried to run.

Selfish. Selfish. Selfish.

No more.

I needed to make sure I never forgot again. Was never weak again. I crept into Ella's room, not wanting to wake Mum, although her level of snoring meant that was pretty unlikely anyway. Sitting at Ella's desk I reached into her pencil case and removed the compass. I pulled up my left sleeve and, trying not to shake, pushed the point in until I saw the blood flow. Swallowing my screams and tears, I kept going, only stopping when my crude carving had finished. The pain was so much that I kept nearly fainting or puking or both, but I tried to fight it back and focus. Whiskey. Not to numb the pain or anything, but to sterilise the cut. The sting from the whiskey was almost worse that the actual cutting had been. I let out one massive scream and I heard Mum stir but then fall back asleep.

The adrenaline pulsing through me meant I couldn't just sit there. I needed to do something – there and then. Take the first step to rescuing my best friend. Pulling on my sweater, I headed into the warm night air. The air's never not warm now. I thought this'd be a good opportunity to scout the Fence. Look for a weak point to break out. Raf and I had debated – in the early days, before our commitment waned – how best to get into the Wetlands. Obviously, I'm sure if we approached some Ministry bod and said we were volunteering to be resettled to free up land for others, they'd have sent us, gladly. But that wasn't the aim. We needed to get in, find Jack, and get BACK. With no one being any the wiser.

Without destroying our parents' lives and putting them on the list of most suspicious people ever. What happened next, how we'd bring the system down we hadn't figured out yet. But it had to be easier to have only one of us in hiding than all three. So we had to breach the Fence, the question was where?

'By Ella's house,' had been my suggestion. Very few people live round here and the land is so infertile that I thought security would be lax at best. That's as far as our thoughts had gone. We'd just assumed that breaking out would be pretty do-able.

But I guess if people could break out then Fish could break in.

It was about a mile's walk from Ella's back garden. I knew the general direction as Aunty Vicki had pointed it out before – down a grooved track and through gorse that tore at my trousers and drew more blood. I thought I'd struggle to see, but I'd forgotten that the Fence is lit. Always. And so I followed the eerie glow until I was just two roads' widths away and at the edge of the floodlit zone. This was the closest I'd ever been. My eyes took it in: tough interlocking wire the height of a two-storey building, with glaring floodlights and brick towers raised at regular intervals along its length.

The Fence.

I swallowed, trying not to be defeated by it. By its sheer size. By its embodiment of cruelty. There must be a way over. I scanned left and right, up and down. Could I scale it? It was doubtful. And then on top of the Fence itself rose the towering mosquito grids. Like some denser I'd totally forgotten about these. Before I could fall into a deeper despair, my thoughts were interrupted by a quiet, regular beating sound. Feet on dry mud. People, running.

They came into the lit zone on the other side of the Fence and I could make out their faces. A woman, so thin she was little more than an animated skeleton, hands clasping her young son, was sprinting towards the wire. She was fast, running for her life, running for her son's life. Letting go of her son, she took a flying leap, one hand grasping the wire, ready to climb, the other extending downwards to scoop up her waiting child. That's when the electricity first entered her body. There was a short, inhuman scream as her limbs jerked wildly on the wires like an epileptic puppet, followed by stillness and the sickly sweet smell of cooking meat. I gagged. To make it even worse, the little boy wouldn't leave. He just stood there, looking at his mother's body and wailing.

It didn't last long.

As if to make some kind of sick point, a machine gun, it must have been from the tower, started firing, ripping through the air, making the woman's body dance again. 'She's dead. She's already dead,' I started shouting. I couldn't stop shouting. 'Stop it, she's already dead.'

And now her boy was too.

Mum went mental when she saw my arm.

I'd stumbled back from the Fence and was halfway through a shower before she was up. I emerged, eyes swollen from crying and my left arm a bloody mess, to see her face collapse in horror.

She started going off on one about the horrific infections she'd seen what she calls 'troubled girls' get who'd harmed themselves like this. Did I know how many bacteria were just about everywhere? Had I seen someone with septicaemia? Seen someone who had to have their arm amputated? How she thought I was smarter than this. Then I shouted back that I couldn't take it, not now and she finally shut up. I told her about the Fence and she hugged me around my neck. Staple like.

'I'm sorry,' I said weakly. 'It was a stupid thing to do. I sterilised it though.'

Mum clearly didn't trust that me and the whiskey had done a good-enough job and went to get Aunty Vicki's first-aid kit from the bathroom. She swabbed and swabbed the cut with iodine, balanced cotton wool pads on it and then wrapped it with a gauze bandage.

'It's a "J" isn't it?' Mum said quietly.

I nodded.

And then she hugged me again, even tighter than before.

Mum dropped me at Raf's straight from Aunty Vicki's. I had to see him. Like a junkie fix. I snuggled into his arms and then winced as my arm was crushed by his body weight. His eyes narrowed into slits of concern, and then he shifted his weight again and I cried out.

'Noa, let me see,' he commanded.

I rolled up my sleeve and he took a sharp breath when he saw the bloodied bandage. 'What? How did this happen? Who did this to you?' Raf's eyes flashed and his body tensed as if he was preparing to protect me from some invisible danger.

'It's not like that ... I did it to me.'

I knew he had to know more, to see it all, so I peeled back the bandage to expose the now dried black blood of the J. His face was impossible to read and the light in his eyes had dimmed. Flat pools of green and blue. Shaded, cold.

I wanted something from him. Pity, anger, jealousy – for him to punch a wall even – but he wasn't Jack. He was Raf. And his weapon was control.

I tried to put my arm round him, but his body remained tight. It was like hugging a statue.

'So the rescue mission's back on then.' It was a statement rather than a question, his voice calm. Too calm.

I nodded. 'But you don't have to come, Raf. If you're having any second thoughts I get it. You don't have to risk your life too. I know you guys weren't like the best of friends.'

'But he clearly means *everything* to you.'

Long awkward pause.

'Do you want me with you, Noa?' Raf's voice was gentle now and more vulnerable. The control was loosening.

I nodded. 'More than anything.'

'Well then there's no way I'm not coming. We're climbing over the Fence together.'

And then he forgot all about my arm and squeeze hugged me again until I shouted out and we ended up both rolling off the sofa in hysterics.

But we were still no closer to solving our first big problem. The Fence. I told Raf about seeing the woman electrocuted.

'So we can't climb it – we dig under it.'

I told Raf about the machine guns. How I'd figured they must be automated, fitted with some sort of motion detector, as there was no way they'd have enough guards to man each and every tower. If we so much as touched the Fence or moved the ground, they'd mow us down.

'So how does anyone get in and out?'

'They don't.'

'Well they do. They've taken Jack and the other kids who failed there.'

'But that's once a year and we've kind of missed that.'

I tried to focus, to channel all my energies into super-concentration mode in order to spark some new ideas, but none came. Approaching something like despair we sat on the sofa and turned on the telly. It was lunchtime so Mum and Dad were at work. They say ideas can creep into your mind when you're relaxed. That your subconscious is somehow busy working it out and then they pop out and reveal themselves like a weirdly welcome flasher.

We were watching a rerun of *Astronaut Tyrone*, which just seemed rubbish rather than malcly funny as it does when me and Dad watch it together. Halfway through, the programme was interrupted by yet another bulletin. The Ministry's favourite rat man was announcing the 'successful' start of prisoners being shipped to the Wetlands 'removing the need for courts and prisons and thereby freeing more precious land for loyal citizens'.

'What about the need for a fair trial?' Raf half-snorted.

But I wasn't really listening. I was staring at the footage of the trucks leaving for the Wetlands with the dodgiest ever-looking criminals in them (where did they find these guys?) On the side of the truck was the image of a huge wheel with an 'H' stamped over it.

'That's it!' I shouted, pointing at the screen.

'What?' said Raf. 'I don't get it.'

'Those trucks – they're Hicks Transport trucks. Remember I told you that Jack's stepdad owns some big trucking company? Well that's his emblem – those are his trucks. That's how we'll get out.'

In autumn you see these squirrels in People's Park. Not many, but a few round the oldest oak and chestnut trees. They're always busy burying acorns and conkers. They look around massively suspiciously, like they're Opposition members about to attend a meeting or something, and then dig a hole and in goes another tasty morsel for the winter.

Raf and I have turned into squirrels. We've got a master list of stuff we definitely need in order to survive in the Wetlands. So far there's iodine, bandages, mosquito repellent and nets, a knife, water purification tablets, dried food, permanent markers, matches, gloves with those grippy bobbles on the fingers and palms for climbing, a compass and a torch.

The medical stuff isn't too much of an issue as Mum's got loads in a cupboard in the bathroom. She gets extra supplies for free from the Laboratory so I don't think she'd notice if some went. Nets and repellent we can get too as all households are given them in case the mosquito grids fail. The markers we've both got at home. I looked at Raf really weirdly when he first suggested it. I'd only ever used them to draw temporary tattoos on my arms with Daisy. I once did a dolphin that I had to turn into a massive tulip as I'd done its nose so out of proportion. But then he explained – to make marks to keep track of the days. So we didn't lose count. So we made it back in time. It was a pretty good suggestion.

Dried food takes longer. We're trying to take little bits slowly over days – the five days we have left – so it's not too obvious, but I still feel really guilty. Stealing from Mum and Dad. Taking food from them when everything's so tightly rationed anyway. I try and justify it – say that that's what they'd want me to do. But I know it's not true. What they'd want is for me to be leaving for the Third City, to be leaving to study and not on a probable suicide mission that puts them in danger too.

Raf said that we didn't need that much, dried food that is, as we could catch our own food out there. I tried not to laugh. Raf's not normally one of those overly manly guys so when he does go a bit caveman it's pretty hilarious.

'You don't think I could, do you?' He acted all mock hurt.

I couldn't answer him as I was still trying to swallow my laughter.

'OK, come with me right now.'

Raf dragged me to People's Park to – wait for it – show me 'how to catch a pigeon'. It was brilliant. He was the worst!! Creeping up on them like a malc cat and then pouncing at totally the wrong time. The pigeons wouldn't even bother to fly away particularly fast. Like they were more embarrassed by him than scared of him. In the end Raf gave up chasing pigeons and started chasing me instead.

We need lots of dried food.

Raf provided the grippy gloves. His stepdad's into climbing and Raf figured we might need them, I don't know – to climb a tree quickly or scale a cliff or get over the Fence if we somehow manage to disable it or something. We don't really know what we're up against.

I got a compass from Dad. He's really into ancient technology, maybe it makes him feel closer to Uncle Max or something, and he seemed properly keen on the idea of me learning to navigate. I told him that Raf and I might need it to go hiking in the Woods some time. The idea that we might be planning to use it to get by in the Wetlands didn't even cross his mind. He just trusts me. Oh, Dad, I'm sorry. I'm so sorry. He even dug out a book on navigating by stars. Maybe he thought if Raf and I spent our evenings together orienteering we were less likely to be doing … other things. He also taught me the basics of Morse code. Which is pretty interesting but since no one else in the world knows it, probably not the most useful.

Taking the torch, however, almost made me abandon the whole thing. We've only got one torch in the house –

this ancient, wind-up thing. Yesterday morning I took it from the hall cupboard and hid it under my duvet. Wow, the master of concealment. The one good thing about having parents who are really into kids doing chores is that they never tidy my room or make my bed or anything. Anyway, last night, a fuse or something blew and the whole flat was plunged into darkness. Mum went to try and see what had happened but obviously couldn't see anything without a torch. Which wasn't too much of a big deal – until she started blaming Dad. Dad's brilliant but pretty disorganised so when stuff's missing, chances are he's put it somewhere stupid. I think Mum was probably just tired and everyone's pretty tense at the moment what with me about to leave and everything – but she went MENTAL at Dad and he started shouting back that he hadn't touched it and that she shouldn't always blame him and then he stormed out the house. I think that's the first time I've ever seen them properly fight. Mum abandoned fixing the problem till morning and fetched some candles instead. At least I now know where the matches are.

I can't see anything. My vision's turned into a weird haze with a halo of light round the edge and I desperately want to scratch the itch in my eyes but the doctor said this might make part of my cornea fall off. Nice. I'm going straight to bed. Tomorrow perfect vision awaits.

Mum's taken me to have my eyes lasered. It's her and Dad's present to me. They'd always said I had to wait till I was eighteen and 'mature enough' to decide if it was *really* what I wanted. Apparently, what with everything that's happened, they think I'm ready to decide now. Obviously, I said yes please. This might sound really superficial but I'd been properly worried about my eyesight messing up our rescue mission. I couldn't exactly wear contact lenses out there as you need super clean hands to put them in and lenses get scratched and fall out at rubbish moments. Sometimes they even get ripped and a little piece gets stuck in my eye and Mum has to invert my eye-lid with a cotton bud to get it out. Grim. So that left a rescue mission in glasses that make me look really rough and again could just fall off and break leaving me a stranded mole. It's not surprising that there're no stories about massively short-sighted people getting ship-wrecked. *Robinson Crusoe got sand in his contact lenses. And then he accidentally sat on his glasses. And then he died.*

The surgery took less than thirty minutes and I tried not to think of what was going on as the laser cut open my cornea. I tried not to think of Daisy lying on a bed like this as they cut into her brain, trying to 'upgrade' her into a freakoid. Turning her into a vegetable.

Then the laser started its reshaping bit and this smell rose into the air like burning flesh. It was exactly the same smell as the woman on the Fence and I gagged.

Jack's mum is horrific and should never have been allowed anywhere near kids let alone to have one. I went to see her this afternoon. I thought I could snoop around and find out more about Jack's stepdad's trucks, the ones they're transporting the prisoners with.

She only opened the door after I'd rung the bell literally twenty times. I must have interrupted her 3pm gin session.

She looked puzzled and a bit annoyed to see me but quickly tried to adjust her face to *kind and concerned*. She's a rubbish actor.

'Hi, Mrs Hicks,' I said. She's taken her new husband's name. 'I came to say how sorry I am, about Jack I mean…' I could feel tears welling behind my eyes just at the mention of his name. This was going to be harder than I'd thought.

'Yes. Thank you, [pause] Noa.' Oh, my God. I think she actually forgot my name for a minute. 'We're all cut up about it.' But she didn't look that cut up. Unless you count a possibly bigger bra size sliced into her chest. 'I only wish I could have gone with him, but… ' and then her voice trailed off and she gestured limply around herself as if the

door and entrance hall were sufficient reason for her to stay behind.

Bitch.

I hadn't left and clearly wasn't about to so she invited me in. I asked if I could see Jack's room one more time and she said to 'make myself at home' then wandered back into the kitchen, not caring where I went as I knew she wouldn't. I know I was supposed to be hunting for info in the room Jack's stepdad uses as his study, but I couldn't resist going into Jack's room anyway, to be close to his things, to him. I pushed open the door and choked. It had been completely cleaned out. His drawings stripped from the walls. The Florrie Fox poster gone and the hole replastered. I'm not saying she should have kept his room completely untouched like some creepy shrine, but come on!

Anger steeled me. I crept down the hall and pushed on the door to the study. It was unlocked. I guess Jack's stepdad didn't need to worry about his wife poking around – that would require a bit more lucidity, a bit less gin. Where to start? There was a central desk (large, mahogany – our old headteacher, Mr Daniels, had one just like it. Must be the kind that men who have feelings of inadequacy buy to make themselves feel more powerful). It was surrounded by bookshelves full of files and boxes of what looked like receipts. On one wall was a massive chart – all rows and columns with random photos of trucks and

people attached – old movies catch-a-serial-killer style. No legible words on it.

There's that phrase, listening 'with one ear out'. I most definitely had both ears out and on high alert as I riffled through file after file looking for anything relating to prisoner shipment details. Nothing. Damn. I froze as there were footsteps in the hall. Staying frozen until there was the sound of a toilet flush and the footsteps padded back to the kitchen.

I looked round the room. I couldn't give up. The chart caught my eye again. Scanning the rows and columns more closely, it became clear that it was a calendar. There were no recognisable words but certain dates had certain letter combinations on them. It had to be a code. Today and tomorrow were blank but the next square had RX1 written on it.

There was one place I hadn't looked. The desk had a drawer.

I tried it.

Locked.

I peered round the door into the hallway to check Jack's mum wasn't on her way back. In case alcohol was some major laxative. She wasn't. The only sound was the murmur of the TV from the kitchen. I rattled the drawer again. It wouldn't come loose but the fact that there was any movement at all meant that the lock had to be weak. Nothing too high tech. I took a brass letter opener from the top of the desk and ran it along the crack at the top of the drawer. It stuck in the centre. I moved it left and then right again. Click. Tentatively I pulled at the handle. The drawer opened.

And then I found it. At the bottom of the drawer. A file, helpfully labelled 'Prisoner Transport'. The Ministry commends you on your discretion, Mr Hicks. The file contained the address of the transport hub along with drawings and specs of the trucks. Mr Hick's amateur attempts at code were translated.

Next to RX1 was scrawled the departure time and number plate of the truck. It was supposed to have twelve prisoners on it.

In two days time we had to be on it too.

Packing and packed lunches. It sounds like the name of a terrible old-people-bonding movie but it was actually an OK day. No, I'll be honest, a great day.

We leave tomorrow, Monday. My bag's ridiculously full as I've had to pack loads of stuff for my imaginary life at the FES too – my Scribe, writing stuff, uniform.

Mum and Dad both made sure they weren't working so we could spend some 'proper' time together. Mum made a picnic and we took it to People's Park and lay on rugs made out of old curtains. The grass was uneven and there were little boats on the rugs that, if you squinted and defocused your eyes so everything went a bit pixelated, looked like they were actually bobbing up and down. Mum had used a gingerbread-man cutter to cut out perfect little men-shaped sandwiches like she used to when I was really small and a bad eater, and I felt all choked up inside. We then obviously had to eat all the cut-out leftovers – we weren't exactly going to throw them away!

After lunch we played Frisbee and Dad was predictably and reassuringly malc at it – he even ran into a tree at one point – I mean how do you not see a tree? And it took everything inside me to remember why I was doing this. Why I was lying to these people, why I was leaving them.

We talked all afternoon and evening. About everything and nothing. It was perfect. Then I had a bath and when I got out and came back into my room I found Mum sitting on my bed. She seemed a bit stiff, a bit straight and I thought – Oh God, she's looked through my bag, she knows, she knows. But then she cleared her throat and started to speak and I realised she wasn't talking about the Wetlands, she was talking about me and Raf, 'going to be spending more time together' and 'intimacy' and I roared with laughter and relief. I told Mum we didn't need to have THE conversation and she looked even more relieved than I did and gave me a huge hug.

'I love you, Noa-bean.'

'Love you too, Mum. I'm going to miss you so much.'

'Me too, but we'll see each other in two months, at half-term, OK? Dad and I will come and visit then, first chance.'

And then I started crying as the chances of my still being alive in two months let alone being safe back in the Territory were approaching a big fat zero per cent. No one's ever managed what Raf and I are planning. It's like I'll coast along fine and then the reality of what we're doing will hit me like a sucker-punch. Mum looked a bit surprised at quite how upset I was getting. She probably thought I was getting my period or something.

I'd told Mum and Dad it'd be easier on everyone if they didn't walk me to the bus stop as that'd be too similar to before, to when I was getting shipped off to the Waiting Place. They agreed, wanting to spare me any unnecessary pain.

I left our apartment block, weighed down by my stuffed backpack and, my head elsewhere, walked splat into Marcus, our friendly neighbourhood policeman-come-killer.

'Careful, love,' he smiled. 'Can't get to college quick

enough?' All his generation still called it college. FES clearly wasn't that catchy. I forced my lips to curl up in a return smile. Nothing must seem unusual. Nothing report-worthy. Just another student keen to start studying again.

I turned right and walked in the direction of the bus stop, the way Marcus expected me to go. A couple of blocks later I doubled back on myself and snaked down alleys and minor roads to meet Raf at the junction of 2nd and 5th Street. God I was pleased to see him. Be held by him. He kissed me and my fear subsided. We could do this thing. Together we could do anything. Ducking into an alley we riffled through our bags and got out everything that was unnecessary, everything that had been for show. I joked that hours later some people might wander past a random pile of textbooks and uniform and think, 'what the hell?' But Raf said we couldn't leave the stuff out to be discovered like that. That it'd look really weird and suspicious and that someone might report it and then they might look into students going to Greenhaven. So that meant we had to spend the next few minutes pushing everything down through the slats of a drain cover. 'Fundamental Principles of Chemistry' nearly didn't fit and I had to bash it quite a few times with the heel of my shoe before it joined its friends on the way to the sewers.

We also sprayed ourselves head to foot with mosquito

repellent. Who knew what was going to happen at the other end? Otherwise we would be bound to be bitten as soon as we emerged from the truck and that would really suck. Ho Ho.

Getting to Hicks Transport depot wasn't too hard. We had to keep going east for about a mile – down 5th and then right down 12th. I had memorised it from a map. We walked with heads slightly lowered so we'd be less easy to identify on CCTV. And we made sure we walked purposefully. That was the key. Meant we were less likely to be stopped by police. But my heart still went crazy every time we passed one. If they searched our bags, found our survival stuff, they'd label us Opposition in a flash. And we'd seen what they did to Opposition.

The mouth of the depot was a huge iron gate set into a brick wall. An open mouth. Five trucks sat on the tarmac; more were lined up inside – under a domed hangar structure – all with the wheel and 'H' stamped on the side. We were in the right place. We had just under an hour to find the right truck and climb into the storage compartment at the back left that we'd identified on the specs I'd taken from Jack's stepdad's home office desk drawer, before they loaded the prisoners on. The dimensions meant it'd be a tight squeeze but we should definitely both fit, our bags too.

Peering round the edge of the wall we checked the number plates of the outside trucks.

No match.

Damn. Had I messed up? Copied down the information for the wrong day? We had to get inside – into the hangar. But how? We didn't exactly have super-spy training. How was I supposed to do some sort of sprint/combat roll manoeuvre when I could barely manage a somersault? I should have tried harder in gym. And then take out the guards? I didn't know where people's pressure points were and there was no way I was going to be snapping any necks. Just the thought made me want to gag.

'Follow me,' Raf whispered.

'What's the plan?' I whispered back, relieved that he was taking charge, relieved that he knew what to do.

'Don't get stopped.'

Not exactly a master plan.

A deep breath, five steps and we were in through the gate. We walked towards the hangar, hugging the brick wall to the left of the tarmac. No one had spotted us. There were no guards with guns. This was too good to be true.

It was too good to be true.

'Stop!' The voice cut through the air. 'You two. Stop there.' A massive man in a dark blue uniform strode towards us. There was no point running.

'What are you doing on Hicks Transport property?' he asked, picking up his radio, no doubt to call for back-up.

37

Raf opened his mouth, but I prodded him and took over. Tried the only thing that I thought could work.

'We've come to see Mr Hicks,' I said.

He raised an eyebrow.

'I am … was … am best friends with his stepson and I wanted to see how he was holding up with Jack gone and everything.' I put on my most pathetic-looking face. 'Mr Hicks is always someone I've looked up to so much and I want him to remain a role model in my life,' I swallowed. The man in uniform swallowed. He looked a bit, 'What!?!' at me, paused and then radioed Mr Hicks' office. Jack's stepdad's voice, tinny and annoying, came back through the speaker.

'Send them up,' he said.

The man marched us forwards into the hangar. We clanged up a spiral of metal stairs after him and then along an open walkway into the office.

Mr Hicks sat behind another massive desk – how inadequate was this guy? – facing the huge window that overlooked the trucks below. He rose to greet us, sweeping a fat, sweaty hand through his ten remaining hairs before thrusting it in our direction. I tried not to flinch as I shook it. He dismissed the guard and sat down, leaving us standing.

He smiled. A forced, jovial smile.

'Sorry about all the security,' he boomed, clearly unable to judge suitable sound volume as we were only two metres away. 'We're doing some pretty serious stuff here at the moment and … (theatrical look stage left, stage right) … there have been break-ins.'

A strange look flitted across his face and I couldn't meet his eyes. Had he noticed the forced drawer on his desk? Had Jack's mum mentioned my visit? I had visions of him shutting the door and calling the police.

I was readying myself to run when he wrinkled his nose and reached down behind his desk.

'Hot in here, isn't it? I'll just put on a fan.'

I released my breath. He wasn't suspicious, he was just trying to work out why we smelt weird. I guess the mosquito grids mean people aren't that used to being in a smallish room with two people covered in Citronella. He probably thought we were just two fifteen year olds who had yet to discover deodorant.

He was back up again, smile still rigidly in place.

'So, Noa (he dragged out my name like he'd just learnt about syllables: NO-A). How can I help you?'

I blanked. I had been going to ask him about Jack. To pretend to want advice on grief, but I couldn't do it. Couldn't keep using Jack and my real emotions as a pawn like that. But I had to say something. Every second I stayed silent was making our visit look increasingly weird. He was going to start asking questions. Why were we here exactly? Why weren't we already on the bus to Greenhaven? Why were we skulking around trucks on a prisoner transport day?

Raf sensed the vacuum and stepped in.

'Noa, you were saying you wanted to ask Mr Hicks about life at FES, at College,' he prompted.

Mr Hicks puffed out his chest. He'd been to College (years before the TAA when it really wasn't the same level of achievement. Of course he didn't see it like that.) This was something he could 'ED-U-CATE' us about.

Mr Hicks started droning on and I pretended to listen intently, making all the right 'Ahh', 'Yes', 'Uh-huh' noises. Halfway through some spiel about studying hard but not too hard 'heh, heh', I turned to the window to hide a yawn and then it suddenly struck me how high up we were. What a good view of the hangar we had. I kicked Raf and spiralled my hand. An attempt at sign language for turn around. It probably actually means washing machine or something like that but it didn't matter, Raf understood.

Raf wandered over to the window, surveying the fleet of trucks. Mr Hicks' eyes flickered over to him, and a frown criss-crossed his brow. Who was this young upstart ignoring his stories? He opened his mouth.

'Look here…'

'Such an impressive operation you have here, Mr Hicks,' came Raf's voice from the window. Respectful but not creepy. Just the right level of deferential. Brilliant!

The frown vanished and Mr Hicks' chest inflated still further. Any more and he'd pop.

'It's all about having a winner's mindset.' Cue another story.

I had to endure a few more minutes of Mr Hicks reliving his glory days as a (definitely fictional) college football star before Raf broke in again.

'So sorry to interrupt, Sir, but I promised Noa's mother I'd have her back by now so we really should make a move. We have a bus to catch after all!' A sly smile spread across his face and I knew he'd succeeded. He'd found the truck.

Mr Hicks looked relieved.

'Probably best,' he said. 'Another *very* busy day here. Prisoner transport you know.'

We nodded back seriously. We appreciated the burden he bore. The responsibility he shouldered.

Mr Hicks offered to get someone to show us out but I quickly jumped in and said not to bother, not on this *very* busy day. That we were pretty independent and could remember the way out.

I thanked him again, for his 'wisdom' – puke – and we started back along the exposed walkway again, forcing our legs to remain at a normal walking speed when they wanted to run, to jig.

At the top of the spiral stairs where we were definitely out of earshot, Raf whispered, 'It's there. Look! No … follow my finger … right a bit.'

I saw it. At the far side of the hangar, second from the right sat our truck: RX1 3LB.

We reached the bottom of the staircase and looked left, right. None of the guards seemed to be coming in our direction; their attention was elsewhere. Here was our chance. Scuttling across the hangar like a couple of ninja crabs, we reached the truck undetected. We were on fire. We were unstoppable.

But there was no time even to take a breath, let alone celebrate. A shrill bell rang out and suddenly the tarmac was flooded with police. Police with guns. The prisoners were being brought in.

'Quick,' Raf hissed. 'Here.' He was crouched next to the access door for the storage compartment – our home for the next however many hours. I took three deep breaths to calm myself. I've always disliked small enclosed spaces – I think I'm probably borderline claustrophobic. This was going to be difficult. Difficult but do-able. Until it wasn't. Until Raf reached out his hand to open the access door and found it locked.

Why had we not thought of this?

I started hyperventilating.

Raf grabbed me.

'Get under the truck.' We hit the ground and scrambled out of sight. Raf riffled through his bag.

'What are you doing?' I whispered. 'Have you got some sort of spanner or...' hope bubbled up, 'a skeleton key?'

He didn't answer me but instead pulled out two pairs of grippy gloves.

'Put them on,' he instructed.

I looked at him. I knew what he was thinking and my legs were already shaking. 'No!' was all I could manage.

'Yes.' He swallowed. 'We have no choice. Now we find somewhere to hang on.'

We'd had seconds to get into position, bodies facing the undercarriage, hands wrapped round pipes, arms extended so we could peer out at an upside-down world, when the prisoners were marched across the hangar towards the truck.

They were flanked on either side by police, well some special branch of the police or army anyway. They wore chunky boots instead of shoes and the jackets had squarer shoulders. Most of the prisoners looked pitiful, a sorry mix of men and women. Thin to the point of being shrunk and with no light in their faces, as if all hope and spark had been sucked out – like those vacuum storage bags that remove the air so suddenly your entire wardrobe fits in. Anger burned in me. These guys were clearly no violent criminals. They were minor Opposition, people who had dared to challenge the system. People who could now be disappeared without trial. But the prisoner at the back was different. He hadn't been shrunk. He looked like the type they showed on telly to justify what they were doing. He had predator written all over his face. His face. He turned and I gagged. It was like the left side had been melted away. The skin was white with weird marks like dripping wax and the ear on that side was little more than a fleshy stump. He said something to the policeman next to him. I don't know what, but it made the policeman mad enough to hit him to the ground with his baton. The guy just laughed though. Rolled around on the ground like it was the best joke ever and he wouldn't stop. Till he did. Till he looked straight under the lorry and his eyes clocked mine. My heart nearly exploded. That was it. We were found already. Raf had seen it too as I felt his whole body tense up next to mine. But the guy didn't call out. He didn't say anything. He just kept eye contact and slowly, ever so slowly, licked his lips.

Travelling at speed clinging to the underneath of a truck that also happens to contain a psycho is about as hard and stupid as it sounds.

Even with the gloves on, my fingers kept nearly slipping off and the metal rods we hung from grew hotter and hotter as the engine ran. Raf next to me, the feeling of his body pressed next to mine, was the only thing that kept me going. Kept me holding on when my muscles were spasming and fingers burning. The thoughts that kept flooding my brain were the worst. The road surface was only a hand span away from my head. From the base of my skull. And it roared and it spat gravel up at us. And the word skull made me think of skeletons and roadkill. If I slipped I'd be roadkill like those squashed foxes you'd occasionally see by the side of the road with their guts steamrollered to the outside of their body.

This was it. This was real and there was no going back.

We knew we were approaching the Fence long before we saw it, not that that's saying much as by now it was dusk and you don't exactly get an excellent view out from underneath a truck. We smelt and tasted the salt in the air and felt the vibrations of the truck lessen as it slowed on the smaller roads. The roads were bumpier here and at one point Raf was nearly thrown as his left shoe was bumped out of its foothold and his left leg dragged along the floor for three seconds before he managed to pull it back up again. The air was becoming lighter. A white harsh artificial light. We were entering the floodlit zone.

I could hardly breathe. I was terrified the light would expose us. That it would momentarily disobey all the laws of Physics and curve round under the truck, announcing our presence to the hundreds of armed guards that my brain insisted would suddenly appear. Images assaulted me. The woman's body on the Fence. Dancing. Cooking.

But the shouts of discovery didn't come and the truck kept going, slowly bouncing along the uneven ground.

Finally it came to a complete stop and we heard this series of hollow clangs, like an enormous, out-of-tune xylophone being hit, and then harsh grinding. The gate to the Fence was being opened. The glare from the floodlights was so intense we had to squint to look out. Then we were on the move again, rumbling through the open gate. We were here. We were in the Wetlands. The truck paused again and I started getting heart palpitations. Everyone knew they scanned the trucks on their way out of the Wetlands. All over – secret compartments, the underneath included. They'd made a big deal about this on the news a while back to show how on top of security the Ministry was. No undesirables getting back in thank you very much. They sent the trucks to a special 'heart-beat' monitor shed to check for stowaways. There hadn't been any mention of scans on the way *into* the Wetlands so we'd assumed we'd be fine. But what if they'd changed protocol? What if they were now doing it this way too? We'd be discovered in seconds. But then the truck rumbled on and I breathed again.

We bumped and jolted our way down a potholed road, deeper into the interior before coming to a complete stop five minutes later. A shrill bell rang and we heard the sound of heavy boots on tarmac and then a metallic click and grind. The guards must have been opening the doors at the back. This was it. We had to run. Without being seen. We peeled our fingers off the pipes and lowered ourselves to the floor. I almost bit off my tongue trying not to scream as I uncurled my now bird-claw-like hands. The gloves were shredded from friction and my fingers were raw and swollen underneath. The prisoners were being taken to the right side of the truck so the left was our only chance of concealment. Crouched with our backs to the truck's side, we scanned the surroundings, looking for a place to flee to. Looking for cover. We'd counted five pairs of heavy boots: five guards. Five guards and twelve prisoners. We had to make ourselves invisible to seventeen people.

A shout and movement. The prisoners were unshackled and on the move. Eleven heading in a row, deeper into the Wetlands. Their step was synchronised, as if still bound together, this time by a shared fear or perhaps a primal instinct that a pack has a better chance of survival. And they followed the old road. Maybe they thought it'd take them to civilisation. But where was the twelfth? Where was the psycho? I risked another glance under the truck and saw him – sat on a raised grassy patch, a smile sliced across his face. The guards clearly didn't get it. Didn't know what he was waiting for. Didn't know it wasn't a what but a who. He started singing to himself. 'Girls and boys come out to play…'

I prodded Raf in the ribs. We needed a plan and my

mind was empty. He looked back. He had nothing too. Was this it? Was this as far as we were going to get? Was this when the guards caught us and interrogated us and then caught our family and everyone I loved became a Fish?

My spiralling thoughts were broken by a groan and then a laugh. Raf and I both hit the floor to see what was happening. The guards, all four of them, had clearly had enough of the psycho too. They'd surrounded him, and were clubbing him. And he just laughed. He kept on laughing.

This was our chance. Scanning left and right. We needed cover. Where the hell do you hide in a salt marsh? Raf tugged my sleeve. There, about a hundred metres to the back left was a raised mound topped with some sort of shrubs. We sprinted to it, ducking low, stabs of pain shooting up through my legs which were shaking and bloodied from the trip, the sound of messed-up laughter chasing at our heels.

You know when you've imagined a place all your life. It's been lurking in the background of every exam you've ever sat, stalked your dreams and shaded every insult you've ever suffered – Fish, Fish, Fish. And now you're here. It's impossible to take in.

After what seemed like hours but was probably only twenty minutes of hiding in the middle of a painfully prickly shrub we braved it and crawled out, crouched, then stood. We were like the lame tableau of the Evolution of Man they've got in City Hall. From the top of our mound we got to look around properly in the last of the day's light and we could see for miles. Guards, truck, psycho all gone. We had the place to ourselves.

I'd imagined total flatness. A flat, shallow sea of death with clouds of mosquitoes. Sea, salt, maybe a few grey-leaved plants like at Aunty Vicki's, but not much more.

I'd been so wrong.

I know we were still pretty close to the Fence but the land here wasn't completely pancake like. There were some weird, crater-style holes like we were on the surface of the moon or something. Then, in the distance we could make out a number of hills ranging from small mounds like the one we were on to proper hike-up hills. One where the last of the sun was setting, so west I guess, and then some more heading to the east. And it wasn't even totally flooded where we were. More like wet in patches but mainly dry sandy earth covered in plants and stuff. Not stuff that we could necessarily eat, but grasses and reeds and patches of fleshy leaves that looked a bit like inflated rubber. And there were animals. When we threw ourselves onto the ground behind the shrub, a small brown animal, a rabbit I think, scampered out the other side and disappeared into the grass. The air even smelt nice. Patches of sea lavender scenting the surroundings like Daisy's mum's pot pourri.

But there was one glaring thing missing. People. In our discussions there'd always been, I don't know, like one big settlement of people which we'd spot immediately and head to and get Jack. And we'd assumed that they'd be near the Fence, 'cos surely that would be where the best land was, right? Furthest from the sea. But there wasn't any settlement. There weren't even any old buildings. One area was scattered with bricks and rubble as if something had stood there years ago, but whatever it had been was now razed to the ground. My stomach should have flipped but actually did this horrific growl. It knew we hadn't eaten for hours even if the rest of my body seemed happy running on concentrated adrenaline. Raf reached for his backpack, wincing as it touched his mangled hands and I smiled, thinking he'd read my mind, smugly thinking that we must be massively in love as we'd developed Mum and Dad's psychic gift, but he actually pulled out a roll of bandage and a bottle of iodine so it seems his mind is both more practical and less romantic and greedy than mine. Raf would make an excellent nurse. Careful, gentle, precise. My hands looked professionally bandaged, almost like I was wearing slim-fitting white gloves whereas my handiwork on him looked ridiculous – more like an escaped mummy from an Egyptian tomb.

The feast then began – a mucor protein bar and bottled water. Mmmm Hmmm. We probably should have only had a little bit of the water, but we were exhausted and dehydrated from our death-trap journey, and figured we had water purification tablets with us anyway. You grow up thinking water doesn't have a taste. It's just there – the least interesting but most available option. But it does, have a taste that is – sweet, soft, clear. Water might actually be the most delicately delicious drink in the world.

Mucor, on the other hand, still tastes like mucor, however hungry you are. We didn't talk – just sipped and chewed and I guess recovered. Eventually, Raf broke the silence and said, 'Rather than trying to spot people, seek out dots on the horizon, we should just ask ourselves, right?'

'Ask ourselves what?' I don't think I was being a denser. I don't think he'd actually asked a question other than to himself, in his head.

'Sorry, what I mean is – where would you go if you had to live here?'

I thought for a minute and then it seemed really obvious.

'Up a hill.'

And then the wolf grin spread over Raf's face and I thought this guy could take me anywhere in the world and I'd feel safe. Or not safe; but not safe in a really good way.

In what seemed like seconds all the light had gone and it was suddenly completely dark. The sliver of moon did almost nothing but then ours eyes adjusted and the stars were awesome. A proper canopy and it seemed like they were just for us. I'd done some reading up from Dad's star book so I pointed out Orion's belt and The Plough.

'What about that star. The really bright one?' asked Raf adjusting position so that his head rested on my stomach.

'Hmmm, maybe Venus. Or the North Star?' I tried to concentrate but kept worrying that my stomach was making weird rumbling sounds straight into Raf's ears. 'I think if it flickers it's a star but if it doesn't it's a planet. Or maybe it's the other way round.'

'Thank you, Professor Blake. This is clearly a subject you know a lot about.'

I poked him in the ribs and he rolled off me, laughing.

'Now come here,' he instructed. 'Put your head here,' he said tapping his shoulder, 'it's my turn to ED-U-CATE you.' He mimicked Mr Hicks so perfectly and his booming voice seemed to bounce around the stillness of the night. We both froze for a few seconds, fearful we'd announced our presence to the world. No one came.

'Sorry about that. Now, this is what I wanted to show you. Look at that constellation … the one that looks like

a tick … yes, that one. That's the Noa's smile constellation.'
And then he totally cracked up at his own hilariousness.
Just because the right hand side of my mouth lifts up more
than the left when I smile. No idea why. It's like the
muscles on the right are stronger. Or I had a mini stroke
as a child. Raf hadn't noticed it till I pointed it out a few
weeks ago and now he claims it's 'adorable' yet clearly also
a bit funny.

'Shut up!' I hissed at him, rising onto my knees in semi-
pretend outrage, totally failing to keep the laughter out of
my voice.

'Make me!' he countered, rising too. 'Come on, I'm still
talking – blah blah blah – and you're completely failing to
make me stop.' He was edging closer and closer until he
was leaning over me, centimetres from my face. 'Can't
think of anything?' he said, teeth white in the near-dark.
Run, little Red Riding Hood, run.

'OK, guess I'd better take care of things myself.' And
then he leant down and kissed me and I forgot all about
the stars and the Wetlands and the psycho and everything.

We decided to camp where we were for the night and
then head out at first light. Although we'd obviously
practised putting up mosquito nets at home during City-
wide drills, it turns out it's loads harder when you don't have
special hooks drilled into a wall at the exact right spacing,
but we managed somehow to drape the nets over the
branches, taking excruciating care not to rip them. Just one

rip could be a restaurant door to a mosquito and then, before you know it: bite, suck suck here's some malaria, then R.I.P. We resprayed ourselves with mosquito repellent and then snuggled down next to each other 'to keep warm'. It wasn't cold. I'd been wondering for a while how we'd sleep next to each other. Whether I'd rest my head on his shoulder or he'd wrap one arm round me or we'd spoon, fitting perfectly together. We ended up spooning, Raf lightly kissing the back of my neck. We didn't totally fit perfectly. His body wasn't quite long enough to totally cradle mine but it was still nice. Really nice. And I fell asleep dreaming of the hills. Imagining they were beacons calling us forward. Flaming beacons. The shade of Jack's hair.

I thought we'd wake at dawn with the sunrise, possibly accompanied by birdsong. It didn't exactly work out like that. It was still dark when we were wrenched from sleep. We looked around, bleary eyed and there it came again – BANG and WHIRRRR and then BANG again. A plane's engine. A bomber. No, two. The earth was lit up by the criss-cross of the plane's lights and it shook beneath us as if it were alive and injured. We burrowed deeper into the shrubs. There was nowhere else to go. We were sitting targets. Waiting. Baited breath.

Then the planes' lights grew dimmer and the engine whirr faded.

'They missed us,' I whispered at Raf. There was no one to overhear us, but it *fitted* the mood.

'I don't think they were aiming for us,' he whispered back.

I looked confused, then realising it was too dark for him to see my expression, I murmured a 'What?' instead.

'Think about it,' Raf replied. 'The craters we saw earlier. The fact that no Fish are camping out here. Bombing must be a regular thing, maybe after each shipment of kids or prisoners or whatever. To stop people settling here, right next to the Fence.'

'So they frighten new Fish away? And flatten the buildings so there's nowhere for them to live?'

'Exactly, the last thing the Ministry wants is for a lot of hungry, angry, dispossessed people to mass at the border. It's one thing for people to support shipping kids and prisoners off in the abstract. It's another to have to *see* the suffering.'

'Maybe it's more than that,' I added. 'I mean, if you have a lot of desperate people in one place, how long before they turn into an army?'

We settled back down under our mosquito net. The bombers had served their purpose, they didn't return. But neither did sleep.

Pick a hill, any hill.

We chose the closest one. With nothing to go on, this seemed like as good an option as any. The sort of option Jack might well have taken. We ate at first light, feeling almost crazily alert – one good thing about not resting much is there's no fog of sleep to wait to clear. Breakfast was another mucor bar followed by a shower of mosquito repellent. It stank. We stank. Like some comical advert for a terrible aftershave … introducing '*Repel*' by Noa and Raf. We'd better start catching some fresh food soon though. We've got enough dried rations for 10 days, but it might take us all of the 29 days we have left to find Jack and get back. That's 19 days of foraging. Raf's complete inability to catch a pigeon in People's Park no longer seemed quite as funny.

The new craters seemed to jump out at us in the light. One must have only been a hundred metres away. A hundred metres near.

We started to pack up our things when my hand hit the smooth surface of the marker pen lurking at the bottom of my backpack. I took it out and drew a short line on the right arm of my bag. Raf did the same. It seemed both unnecessary – we were hardly going to lose track of days when we had a strict deadline of 31 – yet essential at the same time. Like a solemn ritual marking the beginning of something. Entering the unknown.

In the morning light we got a better idea of the lie of the land. Most of the hills weren't smooth or a uniform green, grey or brown. They were jagged, with stuff tumbling up or down the sides. Too irregular and crooked to be a geological phenomenon which meant man-made stuff. Shelters. People.

Energised, we set off, scurrying down the mound and hopping over rabbit holes and tiny streams. I was actually sort of enjoying myself, the bombers almost forgotten. That's the thing when terrible stuff happens at night – it sort of feels like a bad dream so fades from memory as a nightmare might. And Raf was too, enjoying himself that is. We didn't talk about it 'cos it seemed pretty inappropriate. Like tapping your foot to a song at a funeral. But I could tell by the glint in his eye and the toothy grins. And I started imagining us living here, 'at one with nature'.

The most direct route to our hill wasn't along one of the old crumbling roads but instead followed a deep stream, which I was pleased about. Seeing the remains of what had been – decaying buildings, roofless barns, signs that led to nowhere and pylons that had long since stopped humming with electricity – gave me the creeps.

We were already running low on water so now seemed like a good time to test out the water purification tablets.

With Raf next to me in case I malced up and drowned, I took off my socks and shoes, rolled up my jeans and waded in. Unlike the festering pond in People's Park the water here was totally clear so you could see straight down to the bed of pebbles fringed by long reeds or weeds, like mermaid's hair. There were pond skaters and even tiny fish. It must have been coming from the Arable Lands or the Woods instead of a city. I put my finger in and tentatively sucked. Sweetness. No salt. No weird deadly chemicals – none that I could taste anyway. Gleefully, I filled up the empty bottles we had, stuck a purification tablet in each and waited for it to fully dissolve. Look at us go!

I clambered out of the water again, only to find Raf starting to take his clothes off. Shoes, socks, jeans, jumper, top – one by one they were unceremoniously thrown down on a flat stone on the river bank. Just his boxers remained. His white body stood out against the green and blue scenery and even though he's not built like, say, Jack is, the ease with which he stood there, totally unembarrassed, made him hotter than ever. It was like watching a weirdly speeded up, non-prancing about strip show. I imagine.

'What?' I tried to keep my voice neutral but it came out as a strangled and squeaky half question.

'Come on. Haven't you always wondered what it'd feel like to jump in a stream? To bathe in fresh water?'

'We haven't got time…' I looked longingly at the water. I'd like to say that all my reservations were due to my fear of falling behind schedule and that the only draw was the freshness of the water. These were definitely my main considerations but I guess ten per cent of my brain was also thinking about the pull of Raf's body versus the not-so-choice underwear I had on. OK maybe twenty per cent. My underwear was all washed-out, 'practical'. Improvisations on the theme of grey. That's all that's available. Maybe it's another Ministry tactic to lower birth rates.

'You're going in, Noa Blake. The only question is whether you want to get your clothes wet.'

By now, Raf had jumped into the river with a yell and I decided to go for it. I undressed, awkwardly at first and then with less and less care before choosing dive bomb as my graceful method of entry. The coldness and the freshness of the water sent shivers through my body and an involuntary 'whoop' came charging out my mouth.

We dried ourselves in the sun, quickly reapplying mosquito repellent, and then kept moving, Raf every now and then whispering a mocking, high-pitched, 'whoop' into my ear.

Just as we were starting to get hungry again, we practically walked into a duck's nest, just sitting there in the long grass. The duck, outraged, took off in a frenzy of quacking and we uncovered four duck eggs. Duck eggs! That's like 20 points in Foraging 101.

'Cool. So let's make a fire.' I couldn't contain my excitement.

'A fire?'

'Scrambled eggs!'

'We don't have time for scrambled eggs, Noa.'

I opened my mouth to protest at the double standards but then bit my tongue. Raf was right now. I'd be right before. We couldn't keep stopping. This wasn't some holiday.

I watched as Raf tapped an egg gently on a stone to crack it and then sucked the raw egg directly into his mouth. Grim. He looked so pleased with himself though. Like he was the chief hunter in the tribe and had brought home a massive buffalo to feed the village. I copied him and managed to control my gag reflex. It was actually less grim than I thought. Slippery and somehow tasteless yet rich at the same time. I had a second and Raf cracked open a second too but then started heaving. There was a baby duckling in it. Not the sweet, yellow, fluffy kind. The grey-weird-embryo-baby-reptile kind. Life and death separated by an eggshell.

Silent now we continued towards the hill. 'Hope Hill' we'd named it, kind of ironically. We'd guessed we'd be there by mid-afternoon. There was a much smaller mound first that looked uninhabited and then Hope Hill probably another couple of hours' walk further. It was difficult to tell exactly though as mist had been building since noon. We didn't get mist in the Territory. Some occasional lowish clouds or the very occasional freakish fog in the winter, but not mist like this. It rolled towards us, coming from the sea I guess, creating this weird muffled landscape. Like when Jack didn't like a painting he'd done, but didn't want to waste the canvas so just whitewashed it.

The sky didn't stay white though. There was a huge but weirdly solitary cloud embedded in it that was moving our way. I looked at Raf who looked back, clearly as confused as I was. We decided to take shelter under one of the few surviving trees and wait the storm out. But it wasn't that sort of storm.

We heard them before we saw them. A high-pitched 'eeeehhhhhhhhhhhhh'.

Mosquitoes.

A swarm of mosquitoes. It's weird when something happens simultaneously to two people that you both have no training for but that you both just instinctively react to in the same way. Raf and I hit the ground and curled into foetal position. Earth mother protect us now. Burying faces, hands, ears, anything exposed and vulnerable under clothed arms to minimise the chance of being bitten. It was four hours since we'd put on the spray. The spray was supposed to be effective for twelve. 99 per cent effective. I felt them brush over me. Felt the wind created by their horrible beating little wings and although my eyes were tightly shut, nothing could shut out the image playing on virtual retinas of them landing on me, piercing me, injecting me with the death they were carrying. I felt like I didn't breathe for the whole time the swarm was over us. I must have, or I'd be dead. But they would have been really shallow breaths, the kind that supply virtually no oxygen to your body. I was light-headed when I finally stood up.

'Take your clothes off,' Raf ordered. 'All of them.' His voice was serious. This wasn't a game. He'd already started stripping himself. He checked me all over, legs, arms, behind my ears, as emotionless as a surgeon and then I checked him.

We hadn't been bitten.

We were safe.

Both shaking, we redressed in silence and then clung to each other.

'I can't ever lose you,' Raf murmured into my ear, his voice not soft but angry. Angry at what he couldn't control.

We are not at one with nature. I hate nature and I think it's going to kill us.

The mosquitoes moved on but the mist stayed, as thick as school custard. We'd stupidly not thought to check the direction of the hill before the mist thickened so we were navigating using an ancient compass and basing everything on guesswork from where we'd sort of remembered things were in relation to the sun back when we were sucking eggs.

What happened next was completely my fault – I just didn't see the ditch in time. One minute my foot was on a firm bit of long sandy grass, the next it (and the rest of me) was at the bottom of a five-foot drop into a deep salty pool. The weight of my backpack must have flipped me over as I landed heavily on my back and groaned as the muscles around my lower spine and right ankle spasmed. Raf, seconds behind, scrambled down to help me up and I knew from the darkening of his eyes that something was wrong.

'Have I broken something?' I asked in a small voice. I didn't want to look down in case there was a super grim bit of bone poking out from my leg or something and the adrenalin was the only thing stopping the pain from kicking in.

'I don't think so.' Raf scanned my body. 'But your backpack's split.' I gingerly eased it off and saw that it had totally ripped open down one side, the contents having tumbled into the pool below. And that wasn't the worst of it. The pressure of the fall had burst open ten of the remaining mucor bars so they were now floating around me – brown slush pumped up with saltwater. Inedible. And my mosquito repellent – the can must have hit a rock as it fell out the pack; there was this big indent on one side and what must have been a minute hole as a shoal of tiny silver bubbles rose from it through the water. Exhaling safety.

I looked at Raf and tried to fight back the tears but they flooded down my face anyway, blurring my vision and turning him into a blue/green-eyed Cyclops. He hugged me close and stroked my hair, telling me we'd transfer everything else to his backpack, that we had enough repellent to share as long as we found Jack quickly, that we could go to half rations and forage more, that he'd get us home.

My ankle was a bit swollen from the fall so Raf wouldn't let me go any further. We found a dry patch of land and made an A frame from long sticks to hang the mosquito net from (or rather Raf did while I sat lamely with my sore leg elevated on a rock). Raf also insisted we had a fire. To dry me out – so I didn't catch some malc cold and slow us down even more. He spent ages collecting all the driest sticks and reeds he could find and then piled them up in a careful pyramid structure. He was sweaty from the effort and his forehead creased from concentration and I fancied him so much just then. He seemed so strong. So primal. But then he opened his backpack and just started swearing and then went and kicked the pile of sticks. Kicked them again and again and again until they were flat and scattered.

The matches had been in my bag.

How do you know when you've reached rock bottom if whenever you think things can't get any worse the world just keeps on pushing you further down?

We felt more hopeful this morning. I was wearing Raf's spare clothes and my damp ones were drying on a gorse bush. The mist had lifted and we could see Hope Hill was pretty close now and the first, smaller mound was just the other side of what looked like a reed bed. The ground was getting wetter and we took off our shoes and rolled our trousers up to switch to wading mode. There was a half submerged, skeletal hedgerow to our right – a sad reminder that this used to be ultimate farming land. The bread basket of Britain. Before the Flood.

Wading is a weird sensation. Your foot lands on a rock

(fine), damp earth (fine), wet slimy reed (grim) and then it occasionally brushes again something that moves or slithers (totally freaky). I've also discovered that my automatic reflex response to this is to freeze. Brilliant. Not to move my foot, run or call for help. No, just to freeze in fear like a denser prey animal right at the bottom of the food chain. I am clearly not cut out for this.

The wind had changed direction overnight and now it was coming from in front of us, heavy with salt and this other smell. Or rather stench. My first thought was, 'Oh, Raf!' but then I saw that he thought it was me and I was immediately all over that with a big fat NO WAY.

The true source of the smell lay twenty metres in front of us. We were right – the first mound wasn't any sort of settlement. It wasn't even a proper hill or earth structure. It was a pile of dead bodies. Young and old, but not old old, no one much older than my parents say, in various stages of decay. Some just seemed frozen stiff, others were covered with terrible sores. As much as we wanted to, we couldn't turn away. Raf bowed his head out of respect and I saw his mouth move in silent prayer. I forced myself to confront the horror and look at the faces, to check Jack wasn't among them. I didn't go rummaging through the corpses or anything sick like that, but I figured his body would be near the top if he was there. A recent addition. As far as I could tell he wasn't and my legs turned to jelly with relief.

Although it was obviously a mass grave these bodies hadn't just been dumped. The pile seemed to have been made with respect. There were flowers on the top, some woven reeds, white stones that had clearly been specially selected and laid in concentric circles round the base and then pile upon pile of sea lavender and flowering yellow gorse. These were people's loved ones. Victims of the Wetlands. Victims of the Ministry. Anger fought sadness. Anger won.

We backed away, heads bowed from respect, determined to get to the Hill as soon as possible, to rescue Jack and plan our next move.

Hope Hill – what a frickin joke.

We reached it well before sunset. The ground was getting properly wet now with saltwater pools everywhere, but we still skip/splashed the last few hundred metres, our bounds increasing as the settlement buildings grew bigger with our approach. My skips were slightly malc as my ankle was still hurting a bit and Raf definitely wouldn't accept that he skipped, 'guys don't skip', but he did, like a little girl. I think it's probably the most joyful movement you can make and we were fairly high on finally getting to our destination. Each splash sounded like a 'Jack' and I pictured myself like some fairy-tale knight coming to rescue him.

By now we could clearly make out the set up. There was a cluster of what looked like teepees made from reeds. Then there was a fence ringing the hill that had been cobbled together from pieces of corrugated steel and wire, wooden fence slats and what might once have been car doors and road signs. This level of defence seemed odd. Maybe there were some particularly hungry foxes or something round here or maybe it kept the water out if it was tidal. Presumably it could be tidal if we were getting closer and closer to the sea proper? Then above the fence was I guess what they used to call a village or maybe a slum. There were a few old buildings, probably a pre-Flood farm, surrounded by lots of makeshift additional shelters made from the same stuff as the base fence. It looked a bit like the images they used to show us at Hollets of refugees living in crowded squalor as they tried to escape the countries whose climates were totally burning up. They used them tell us how lucky we were that we lived in the Territory. How *civilised* we were. Ha.

'Hello!' Our shouts sounded strange against the stillness of the landscape, as out of place as someone shouting in Assembly. We heard movement, the creak of a metal shelter, but no one came out.

'Hello!' we tried again, desperation now seeping in.

'HELLO!' We approached the fence and tried to push one section open.

'Stop there!' shouted a young guy's voice. Hostile, warning. A guard.

I don't know exactly what I'd imagined, but it wasn't this. Actually, who am I kidding? I know exactly what I'd imagined. I'd imagined knocking at some sort of door and it being opened. I'd imagined being welcomed with open arms and an offer of food and shelter. I'd imagined thanking our new hosts, who for some reason were all wearing long velvet cloaks, but explaining that we were here for Jack. And, then, before I'd even finished my explanation, I'd imagined Jack appearing and running towards me – huge, reassuringly ginger – and picking me up and spinning me round and round and saying something like, 'Noa Blake, I presume.' And then I'd imagined us laughing and laughing and me feeling whole again.

None of that happened.

A group of four guys, probably in their twenties and armed with huge sticks and metal bars, appeared at the fence and peeled back a section of metal to speak to or rather confront us. They told us to leave. Said, 'we don't deal with traders here.'

We tried to explain. We weren't traders, whatever they were. I mentioned Jack and said he was on the last shipment of kids out. But they said they hadn't taken anyone from that in. They weren't taking anyone else in. They couldn't support any more people. Round the ankles of one of the men appeared this little girl, thin but with a belly swollen from lack of protein. Kwashiorkor. We'd done it in Biology. Nature's sick joke. The man shook his leg and told her to leave. To, 'Go back to Mum.' Stern but soft. And then I started noticing that the guys weren't that big either. Their anger, their attitude inflated their otherwise thin chests and weak arms.

Raf tugged at my arm. 'Come on, let's go.'

But I couldn't accept it.

'Jack!' I started shouting. It rose to a scream, 'JACK!'

'He's not here,' one of the men shouted back. 'You've got to leave. We need to look after our own.'

And I looked deep into his eyes and saw there was no cruelty there, no deception. Just desperation.

So we left.

Thirst. Horrific, unquenchable thirst. The sort that swells your tongue and sinks your eyes and shrivels your skin. A feral animal that crawls out of your mouth and demands to be fed.

Our bottled water is gone. As are the fresh water streams. Before it hadn't seemed like water'd be an issue.

We'd just kept on filling our bottles from the fast flowing streams and small rivers that cut through the drier land. It was just a question of dunking in our water bottles and popping in a water purification tablet or two. OK, the water hadn't always looked the nicest – once I had an actual snail in my bottle – but it was water and it kept us going. Now that we were deeper into the Wetlands everything had changed. The streams had mixed too much with the saltwater pools so there was nothing fresh left. *Water, water everywhere but not a drop to drink.* It's so hard resisting the temptation to cup your hands and sip just a little. The devil's voice in your ear murmurs, 'A little bit of salt can't hurt you,' and you know it's poison but his whispering gets louder and louder.

Raf is pretending everything's fine. Fine seems to be the only word he knows at the moment. Hope Hill shuts its doors on us. *We'll be fine.* We don't have a clue where we're going now and are basically out of food. *It's fine.* There's no water. *FINE FINE FINE.* It's like he doesn't trust himself to show doubt in front of me. To be vulnerable. To be human.

He said there're loads of sources of water other than actual water. You can suck the stems of fleshy plants, drink the blood of animals and fish. But we haven't found any fleshy plants and we haven't caught any animals or fish. We chased a rabbit for about ten minutes but it managed to disappear into long grass and we couldn't flush it out again.

'If a rabbit can live, we can,' Raf declared, as logical as ever. 'They need water too.' But maybe the rabbit was scampering back to the drier land to drink. Going back isn't an option for us. Or maybe it can last longer. It didn't have weird bloodshot eyes. And I'm pretty sure it doesn't keep on seeing Daisy just up ahead calling to it. Daisy's smile. I think if I could just stop and rest for a while, Daisy would come to me. Hug me. And we could talk like old times. And she could tease me and we could laugh about how I'd thought she'd died.

I must have sat down as the next thing I knew, Raf was pulling me up and shaking me violently. He wouldn't let me stop. He wouldn't let me rest. Every time I tried to sit down, he'd tug me up again under my arms and order me to keep walking. And the time I said I was going to sip from a pool, just a little, he slapped my face and told me to get with it.

We've picked another hill now. Scientifically. We did eeney meeny miny mo. So that's where we're heading. We haven't named it this time. I read somewhere ages ago that ancient cultures didn't name their babies till they were one and a half or two or something. They thought that giving them names showed an arrogant belief that the baby would survive infancy and such arrogance angered the Gods.

When we were nine, me and Daisy found an injured pigeon in People's Park. I think a Police dog must have got it, or maybe it'd been run over by a car. Anyway, one of its wings was broken and mangled so it couldn't fly and couldn't even hop straight. It kept on going round in a circle like a clockwork mouse gone wrong. Daisy was sure we could heal the bird and so she picked it up gently and carried it home wrapped in her jumper, blood seeping into the sleeves. Daisy is … was, a really kind person so would definitely want to help a creature in pain whatever, but I think this time she was actually thinking about the fact that she'd never had a pet, her mum claiming to be allergic to anything with a heartbeat, and now, since Dead Dog day, this was probably the only chance she'd get. We made the bird a 'nest' out of a shoebox filled with shredded cardboard and hid it strategically behind Daisy's coats in her wardrobe. We fed it on worms, grim sounding I know. Yes, we actually dug up worms, mashed them up and served them to Fred the pigeon on a teaspoon. Daisy's mum would have had an epi-fit if she'd found out. Every time she stirred her tea after that I'd get the giggles, thinking that maybe she was using the worm spoon!

The bird didn't make it – two days later Daisy found it

dead. But ever since that moment I've felt a sort of affinity to birds. Like I'm their friend and somehow they know it.

It seemed kind of right then that salvation for me and Raf came in the form of a seagull. I realise it might sound from that like it carried us a message like birds did in the olden days ('fresh water, 200m to the west') or was a sign like a biblical dove, bringing us an olive branch from an irrigated oasis. It didn't and it wasn't. We ate it.

We'd stumbled across it that morning. Literally just outside where we'd made camp. It had been injured – its left wing hung limply at a weird angle – and some of its feathers were blood stained. I had to fight back the memories of me and Daisy. Of happier, easier times.

I don't know if seagulls are supposed to be edible but when you can hardly focus because you're so thirsty and you have one mucor bar left between you, you get pretty experimental. I picked it up and tried to quieten it as it squarked and shrieked and flapped its good wing wildly. I murmured softly to it, trying to calm it, nodding at Raf at the same time. Raf understood. He brought a rock down on its head. He then took a knife from his pack and cut the seagull's neck. He brought it to his lips and sucked, then pulled away disgusted and it was my turn. The blood was warm, thick and metallic and my body made me drink.

After we'd sucked out every drop we could, we plucked the bird and cut up the meagre amount of meat, forcing it down, trying to see it as cubes of energy.

It didn't quench our thirst. There was no miraculous recovery. But we were still alive. We could keep walking.

I have no memory of arriving at the next hill settlement.

I'd felt faint all day. It was hot, really unbearably hot and the heat seemed to be hitting us from two directions – from above obviously, 'cos durrr the sun's in the sky, but also weirdly from below – bouncing back at us, reflected by the pools of water everywhere. We were sunburnt, starving and ridiculously dehydrated. We opened the last mucor bar at breakfast and then this enormous gull swooped down out of nowhere, all hooked yellow beak and dead snake eyes, grabbed the bar in its claws and shot back into the sky. We screamed after it, aware as we did it how totally pointless this was, but anger needs some form of escape valve. Like a boiling kettle.

Part of me accepted it though. Saw it as a kind of seagull justice for what we'd done. But while acceptance might be good for the soul, it does nothing for blood sugar levels. I've always needed regular meals. Mum says I have a 'high metabolism' which supposedly used to be good as it meant you never got fat, but for life in the Territory even let alone out here it's massively annoying as with rationing there's no chance of anyone getting fat and it just means

I'm often just really hungry or am the dizzy special kid who needs to sit down suddenly. I needed to sit down suddenly all morning.

I could see Raf was getting properly worried about me. He wouldn't let me take turns carrying the backpack like normal even though he wasn't doing so well either and clearly needed a break. Near midday the sun was so hot we desperately needed shelter but there wasn't a tree in sight. What there was instead was a crumbling house, an old farm house presumably, with half the roof tiles missing, exposing bare timbers and water up to the level of the first few bricks.

We'd been avoiding buildings, well the ones we'd seen on the way. The ones closer to the Fence had all been flattened. And then other ones had been too flooded or isolated. I'm pretty sure Jack would have headed to a bigger settlement rather than hidden out alone and the single buildings always looked so empty, so lonely that they scared me.

We'd peeped in a few before but there was never any food or bottles of water left in them – the insides always being stripped bare – and I was terrified that we might stumble across the psycho from the bus as he was exactly the sort of freak who would camp out alone and, I don't know, eat people who came past.

We sidled up to the house and peered through the open doorway. Listened. No sight or sound of anyone. There were rusty hinges where the front door had once been – this place had been looted long ago. Splashing through the hall and into the living room I was suddenly filled with terrible sadness. There was a sodden sofa with stuffing ripped out, a painting on the wall of lots of sheep on grass next to a river and a sign over the fireplace – 'welcome to our happy home'. It was the sort of thing that would have made Daisy mime puking but it just really choked me up. It spoke of a different type of people and a different time. A time when people had gardens, sheep walked around eating grass and people put up innocent, sweet, really tacky signs.

The afternoon brought with it a bunch of clouds which calmed the heat a bit so we could set off again. Marching, trying not to lose pace, trying not to think about our thick tongues and throbbing heads.

Just as the hill seemed within reach at last my vision went weird, I have a vague embarrassing memory of calling for Mum and then there was blackness.

'*A bone to the dog is not charity. Charity is the bone shared with the dog, when you are just as hungry as the dog.*'

Jack London said this. He's one of Dad's favourite writers. I've only read *White Fang*, but that was brilliant.

And I think he's totally right on this, charity, not dogs that is. When Amanda's mum used to try to give me Amanda's old clothes she was obviously being really kind and everything, but the guys at this settlement – they're on a different level.

Raf said he'd been terrified that we'd be turned away again. He was carrying me, passed out, as he walked up to the settlement's fence – the same sort of makeshift job as the last one. A sentry appeared again and Raf had a horrific sense of déjà vu. What if we'd been rejected again? That would have been it for us. Dying alone in the Wetlands, not having even found Jack. A stupid, pointless death. But the sentry had fetched a group who walked as if they were in charge, all hips and shoulders, and Raf had explained our situation and begged, literally got on his knees and begged, and they'd let us in. They'd agreed to share their limited supplies with us, complete strangers. One of the group had taken us to a structure at the far end of the settlement and a woman in her twenties had checked us for fever and mosquito bites and then given us water and strips of dried meat. Then we'd been left to sleep. And we must have slept for AGES as when we woke up it was properly day time. A woman, Mary, Raf said it was the one from last night, came to check on us, and give us some weird-smelling mosquito oil. Thank God as we only had enough of ours left to coat one of our hands! Out the window, or rather hole in the wall, we saw loads of people walking in one direction, up the hill. When I asked her where everyone was going she said, 'to eat'. I asked if we could join in breakfast as I was still absolutely starving and she laughed and said. 'Lunch. Sure – you can join in lunch.'

Jack's not here.

Everything had seemed so right, like we were destined to come to this settlement. They'd let us in after all, were caring for us, so I just assumed, why now I have no idea, that Jack would be here. That we'd come to the end of our quest. But he's not. And my heart feels a hundred times heavier. It's now weeks since I watched him being dragged into the cage. Weeks since I promised to come after him. He's going to think I've forgotten him. That my promise was empty, counted for nothing.

I scanned the entire food hall – well barn, 'The Barn' they call it – and not a red head in sight. I started walking round asking everyone, 'Have you seen Jack? Jack Munro? He's really tall with bright orange hair?' I think I must have started acting a bit like a crazy lady as one of the girls, just a few years older than us, pulled me aside and told me to talk to Annie, who I guess must be the group's leader.

I found her in a shed on the other side of the

settlement. Milking a cow! I had no idea there were still cows around but Annie, laughing at my stunned denser face, told me there were still a few roaming wild over drier sections of the Wetlands. They were like the most valuable things ever – for their milk and everything – so they had to be kept inside the settlement to protect them from Raiders. This cow's name was Brian. The kids who found her had never seen a cow before, Annie laughed, so they didn't know the udders meant it was a girl. You can tell from Annie's face that she laughs a lot. I liked her immediately.

I did a mental rewind of what had just been said. Raiders? There was so much new stuff being thrown at me that I must have looked like a living, breathing question mark.

I don't think I really wanted the answers though. Annie confirmed my worst fears.

Jack wasn't here. They'd let in four students this time, with the six parents that had come with them. Ten's their maximum intake at any one time, there's no way they could fit and feed anymore. But there was no one called Jack. No one with red hair. 'It doesn't mean he's not safe,' Annie reassured me. 'It just means he's not here.'

The Raiders explain the fences and the lookouts. Apparently there's no pattern to their coming. They might come two nights in a row or months might go by without an attack. Annie said they came for supplies, animals and she seemed to be about to say something else but then she drew her mouth into a tight line instead.

'But who would do that?' I asked, furious that someone would steal from these amazing, kind people. Surely if everyone in the Wetlands had been kicked out the territory they'd be a sense of shared destiny. My enemy's enemy and so on.

'For some civilisation is just a mask,' Annie replied sadly, sounding like this English teacher I used to have in year 8 when we did *Lord of the Flies*. The Ministry seems to like books where bad stuff happens to kids. 'Take it away and there is nothing but darkness.' I remember Dad talking about the Dark Days and Uncle Max and shuddered. They'd seen the darkness.

'That's why what we're doing here is so important,' Annie continued. 'Just continuing to live, to survive is not enough. Some settlements out here have turned insular. They live in fear of Raiders, of outsiders, so they don't trade, they don't educate, they don't interact in anyway with the outside world.' I thought of the first settlement we'd been to. The lean, desperate faces. 'We need to think about the sort of society we want to build and the sort of values we want it to have. We can see this exile, the Wetlands themselves, as an opportunity to build a better world than that of the Territory. A world of humanity not just humans.'

This silence lay between us, but it wasn't one of those

empty, awkward sort of silences. It was a pregnant silence, full of quiet optimism.

'I know it takes some adjusting at first,' Annie continued, her voice soft. 'But you can learn to live out here. And the more people who embrace our ways, the fewer recruits the Raiders will get. We will overcome them.'

Annie glanced up at the sun. 'Now, the afternoon's running away from us. You and the boy you came with are on water duty.'

'I'm sorry but I have to leave,' I explained. 'I have to find Jack.'

'When you're stronger.'

I started to protest but was instantly cut off – by Annie's voice and my already buckling knees. God, I'm a weakling now.

'No arguments. You won't last the journey. Rest here a week. You'll help, but nothing too strenuous, and we'll teach you how to survive. We'll ask any passing traders if they have information. Then you can find your friend. Ben will take you to the water purifiers.'

And there was something so calming about the way Annie spoke and took charge that I didn't argue any more. I wonder if she'd been some sort of doctor or healer back in the Territory. Not some bogus crystal gazer or anything but someone who was just totally OK with their place in the universe.

My curiosity ate at me so I turned back to ask her.

'We try not to talk of the past here,' Annie replied, a smile softening her refusal to answer. 'If you look back you stay trapped. We have to look forward. Always forward.'

The water purifiers were a revelation. Just beyond their perimeter fence was a collection of big old baths and tanks and what were probably old animal feeding troughs covered in tarpaulin. Ben, lanky with gapped grin of a face and tight afro curls, explained how it worked and it was genius. You fill the bath/tank half full of saltwater and put a smaller empty pot inside (taking care that no saltwater gets in it). You then tie a tarp tightly over the top and put a big stone on the tarp just above where the empty container is. Then leave it for 24 hours. The pure water evaporates off in the heat, leaving the salt bit behind. The vapour then hits the tarp where it cools and condenses. The drops pour down where the tarp is depressed by the rock so they drip into the empty container filling it with pure water. The system had been invented by one of the first recruits, Matt. I said something like, 'I thought the Ministry made it really difficult for scientists to leave the Territory.' Ben seemed to find this hilarious and his face turned into a massive pair of dimples and white teeth. I could have fitted my little finger in the gap between his front two. I didn't obviously because that would have been really weird, but once the thought had entered my mind it was difficult to shake.

'Matt's not a scientist,' he managed to get out between spluttering laughs. 'I probably shouldn't go into this, you know, 'cos people don't really talk much about life before. It's not best not to dwell, you know?' Then his laughter stopped and I caught a flicker of sadness in Ben's eyes. Maybe a chasm is a better word for it. A sadness so deep that I wondered what he'd seen. What he'd suffered. Everyone here must have their own private abyss.

Ben gave a little head shake before continuing, like a wet dog, but I guess it was memories rather than water he was getting rid of.

'Matt's just a normal kid. He failed the TAA something like six years ago now and came out here with his dad who was a priest. Quite a high-up priest I think.'

Here's where I was worried that Ben was going to say Matt had been shown the way by God in a miracle and it was going to turn out that we'd stumbled into some weirdo cult town. But he didn't. Apparently Matt had got the idea just by watching water drops condense on part of the metal fence that was sticking out of a saltwater pool one hot day. He'd tasted the drops, realised it was pure water, and a few weeks of experimenting later, had come up with the bath-tub design. They'd then traded the design with other settlements in exchange for information on superior seaweed drying techniques and so on. Matt was on some trading mission now.

'With his dad?'

'No, his dad died from malaria a couple of years back. Now, let me show you the salt pools.' And there it was – death of someone's parent to salt pools without breaking stride. Death out here was mundane, expected. Like rain or the occasional cold. I caught Raf's eye and saw that he'd noticed it too and been humbled by it.

Apart from carrying the buckets over to the salt pools and lugging them back full to start the whole process, the work wasn't that hard. And it was nice to have a task. A doable task that your brain can focus on. It seemed to shut down all that other background chatter going on in my head. And looking at Raf, I could see that he needed it too. The worry lines started to soften in his face, as if it was being ironed, and he even kissed me mid-task. And it was only when we kissed that I realised we hadn't done this for days and I'd missed it so much.

Sometimes a tiny bit of food when you're really hungry just makes you feel hungrier. I think it's the same with information.

I made it my mission to hunt down the four kids that had been taken in just before us, to see if by any miracle they'd met Jack and had any news of him. It was dinner time and they were sitting together in the Barn. Sea kelp and fish all round. It was actually delicious. The group on food duty had gone fishing instead of hunting today and said the sea trout had basically leapt into their hands. I felt a bit weird eating it, but everyone assured us that fish out here is safe. That the salt in the brackish streams stopped any of the evil bacteria growing. And fresh fish was an extra special treat, we were told. Normally it's the stored and salted type. I looked at the four kids more closely. None of them had been at Hollets. I started interrogating them. None had walked this way with Jack. I was getting that sinking, drowning feeling again when one of them, Mike, suddenly looked up. He was clearly a bit of a slow thinker as you could see the memory sort of drift across his forehead and the rusty cogs turn.

'Tall and ginger with a bashed-up body?'

My heart literally stopped beating. Someone had seen Jack. I felt this stupid, intense jealousy that Mike had seen Jack and not me and had to fight it back into the reptile part of my brain. Mike said everyone who failed got taken to a Holding Centre after the Waiting Place and then they got bussed out from there. It was at the Holding Centre that Mike had talked to Jack. He'd noticed him 'cos Jack had looked so wrecked – Mike had been worried that the guards were massively violent and would beat him up next. Jack had apparently laughed and said the guards were sadists but that wasn't how it happened.

'How did it happen?' Mike had asked.

'...Let's just call it girl trouble,' was Jack's answer.

'Seriously? Hope she was worth it.' Mike had been incredulous.

'She was. She is,' Jack had replied.

They didn't get put on the same bus so Mike has no idea where Jack would have gone when he got to the Wetlands. What direction he went in.

And that's all I know.

But I went to bed with the words, 'She was. She is,' ringing in my ears.

Day two at the Peak – that's what everyone here calls the settlement, and it started with a shower. Well, a marker pen line on Raf's bag and then a shower. Raf and me are now sleeping in one of the bigger older buildings. It's basically a dorm for people without family. The morning bell rang and I pulled on my clothes (under my blanket – I'm still not used to all this public living) and started heading towards the Barn for breakfast. Sam, who seems to be head of dorm, grabbed my arm as I passed him.

'Showers first,' he said and pointed towards an iron shack down a path to the left.

It seemed more like an instruction than an invitation, but I wasn't about to complain. I approached the shed eagerly. A shower! They had managed to invent some genius way of purifying water so my brain was racing with images of solar-powered hot water and shower gel made from the extract of some local shrub. I'm a denser. The 'showers' involved standing naked in a small shed while someone threw a bucket of salt water over you and then someone else passed you a strip of what looked like and probably was old curtain to dry yourself. At least there were separate men's and women's.

I must have got some ridiculous expression on when I came out as Raf emerged at pretty much the same time, took one look at me and cracked up.

'What did you expect?' he teased. I obviously didn't tell him. I did tell him about the pervy girl who watched me 'shower' and dry. Raf said it was the same in the men's, but they weren't being pervs. They were meant to be there. To check for mosquito bites. To see if anyone needed quarantining. In case they hadn't self-declared. Although the air outside was warm and the strip of curtain/towel had dried off most of the water, I still shivered.

I'm now a teacher! Well, assistant teacher. Annie's assigned me to help with the kids. School's compulsory here for everyone under twelve, after which you start helping with all the different jobs that keep this place going.

I feel really old in the role of teacher. And that's one weird thing I've noticed. There really aren't many old people at all. A few younger kids, loads of teens and people in their twenties but then it really tails off. Not much in the way of grey hair and without hair dye and plastic surgery high on the list of priorities you can be pretty sure there aren't any ancients in camouflage.

I asked Ben about this at breakfast, 'cos I'd expected more, oldies that is. I know some parents of kids who fail do selfishly choose to stay in the Territory but a significant number do come. I mean six came with the four kids who arrived most recently. So where were they all? Ben was quiet for a while then mumbled something about the older ones finding it harder to adapt. They were more likely to forget their mosquito repellent or couldn't handle the raids, the foraging for food and stuff. Ben's dad had only lasted four years, he said. His mum was still here though. She was the school's headmistress he said proudly.

There are seventeen kids in the school. What's crazy is that means they've all been born out here so this is life as they know it and I can't quite imagine what that must be like. Never to have seen a light bulb, been to a shop, seen 360 degrees of dry land or gone to a school with actual desks. I was worried they might be like some sort of vicious feral animal, and they did look a bit scary at first in their clothes sewn together from old material or curtains or sofa covers – whatever had been salvaged from the old buildings. But they were still basically kids, kids who'd seen too much fear and death. That is not something you should get used to.

Maggie, that's Ben's mum, introduced me to the class. The lessons were in the Barn after breakfast had been cleared away. I thought the lessons would be just on, I don't know, fire building, water purification, edible plant identification, that sort of thing, but while that was obviously stressed, there was way more than that. There was Storytelling, Maths for trading and working out if we had enough supplies, Art with different coloured clays being painted onto canvases made from plaited dried reeds, Music from wooden instruments that looked a bit like recorders gone wrong and singing. I was blown away. I asked Maggie about it.

'What's the point of this?' I said. I'm embarrassed by my question now, but that's what I said. Maggie wasn't offended. Amused if anything. 'Why teach Art and Stories at all?' I blundered on. 'They're not exactly going to have lots of books to read or galleries to go to. Why not just focus on survival? And then, why even have school? Couldn't they just follow the older ones around and learn how to do things, like I'm doing with Ben and you?'

Maggie said it came back down to what Annie had said. Humanity not just humans. Otherwise what were we surviving for?

'And what could be more precious or worth saving than childhood?'

And the kids were great. The idea of learning being fun seemed as weird to me as an alien language. *We come in peace x^2 minus three and the life cycle of plasmodium.* At Hollets you learnt stuff to pass exams. You didn't care about the content, you just tried to cram it into your head and hoped that the next nugget of knowledge wouldn't push another fact out. But these kids seemed to like school. Maybe even love it. And not because they were complete losers or had a lead plugged into the back of their neck brainwashing them, but because I guess stuff can actually be really interesting when you're not then going to sit a life-or-death exam on it. OK, so they weren't saints or anything. They often talked over the teacher and one girl spent so much time drooling over this boy that she clearly had a massive crush on that it was embarrassing, but the overall atmosphere was different.

Talking of different, one of the girls, Cara, had this super strange look I've never seen before. Her skin was really chalky white and her hair was white too. Not ash blonde or white blonde or even bleached blonde. Just white. Which doesn't make any sense in an eleven year old. From the back, you'd think she was a skinny little old lady who happened to be into skipping. I thought that maybe she was an albino. At school we once had a pair of albino mice in the lab. Come to think of it, Mum's work always used albino mice too, maybe because white mice seem somehow cleaner and more scientific than grey mice and less like you've just found them in a trap spreading disease in someone's kitchen. But the albino mice had bright pink eyes and Cara's eyes are green.

Cara kept checking her watch and then left the lesson halfway through. No one seemed to think this was unusual. She didn't even ask Maggie for permission and it wasn't like she sneaked out or anything as Maggie turned to look at her and nodded goodbye. And this is when it gets even weirder – a few minutes later she was replaced by a boy, Elias, who looked like he had bleached olive skin and a shock of curly white hair. I tried to ask Maggie about them but she got all angsty and clearly didn't want to talk about it.

'Please don't tell anyone when you leave,' was all she'd say, a tremor of emotion in her voice. 'Don't tell anyone they're here.'

I didn't see Raf till dinner in the Barn. It was the longest we'd been apart for ages so I literally tore over to him and flung myself around his neck. He didn't even look embarrassed, he just grinned right back at me, all semi-tame wolf. And then we just talked and talked about our days, both so excited.

Raf'd been on mosquito repellent duty. Apparently mosquitoes don't like the smell of lavender. Crazy, I know. Lavender, urrghhh yuck whereas blood, mmmm mmmm. He and this girl Emma and three others had spent the morning collecting loads of sea lavender growing in an area about an hour's walk from the Peak. Raf said it had been properly beautiful. From a distance the ground had looked purple there was so many flowers, and the air was just like inhaling a scented candle.

'Sounds amazing!'

'The collecting bit was awesome but the actual making bit was grim.' But Raf's massive grin told me that, grim or not, he'd loved it.

They'd had to build a fire using this cool timber box thing and then they made a big vat of oil by melting animal fat, mainly stripped from seagulls and rabbits – there aren't exactly any essential oils available! The lavender flowers are then added to the oil and stirred around with a massive stick. The lavender oil which contains the smell bit then enters the animal oil and hey presto – mosquito repellent! Raf's eyes were sparkling at the sheer ingenuity of it all. He was just buzzing.

They poured the finished product into bottles and every house, well shack, got one. He'd had to deliver them at the end of the day. Although what had been a bit strange, he'd said, was that when he knocked at the entrance to the iron shack three doors down from the Barn, this girl, aged about ten, had answered with a shy smile that she didn't need any repellent thank you. I said that maybe she'd got an extra bottle last time, or maybe she hadn't understood properly. I mean ten's still quite young, but Raf wasn't convinced. He said there was something a bit different about the girl.

'This is going to sound stupid and it was probably because it was dark in the doorway and everything but she looked like she had completely white hair.'

I jumped in there with details of my school day and Cara and Elias but was quickly distracted by Ben coming over.

Ben said that tonight Raf and I get our own shack. I'm so excited. The two guys who normally sleep there have gone on an 'extended foraging trip', which basically means they're searching for bigger animals like sheep or cows or even beached dolphins, so we've been allocated it. There's padding on the floor that's going to feel like absolute luxury, and even proper hooks for hanging our mosquito nets.

'Space to … move around,' Raf said with a wink and a squeeze of my hand. Oh my God. I think we're going to actually do it. I'm pretty sure that's what Raf was meaning. I knew this moment would come, but I'm not sure that

I'm quite ready, which sounds crazy as I'm crazy about this guy.

Then I thought of an obstacle. An end-of-discussion obstacle. 'We don't have any … you know, well, you know…'

Raf's answer was to riffle around in his backpack and pull out a condom. My face must have been all WHAT?!! How presumptuous are you!?!?!?!?!?! Because he had the good grace to turn bright red and look super embarrassed.

'It's not what it seems,' he spluttered.

'Really?'

'They're supposed to be really useful as part of a survival kit. They can carry up to two litres of water, keep kindling dry and form the elastic part of a catapult.'

We hadn't used them for any of that but still, I had to give it to him for ingenuity.

I think Daisy would say 'go for it' as that was her motto for life, but that was about snogging. This is a far bigger step.

In books and movies sex with someone for the first time is always amazing. Particularly if you love them. This magical experience where your bodies meld together and you get carried to heavenly planes of ecstatic bliss.

I hate books and movies. They LIE LIE LIE! Sex for the first time is rubbish. It's awkward and painful and embarrassing. Nothing fits, you don't know what to do or how to move and you're so worried that the other person thinks you're a right amateur that the chance of actually enjoying yourself is less than zero. Either that or it's just me and I'm rubbish at sex. Either way – aagggggghhhhh!

Raf and me didn't even talk about it afterwards. We just sort of said a really tense goodnight and turned away from each other to sleep, or in my case lie there with my mind running a million miles an hour.

I wish I had Daisy to talk to. Mum even. Not Dad. Dad would slam his hands over his ears and hum really loudly so he didn't have to hear. That, or go and kill Raf. Mum would find it really embarrassing and be biting her tongue trying not to yell at me for sleeping with someone, but she'd still care and give me a hug and tell me everything was going to be alright.

It's the middle of the night and I'm lying next to Raf and I've never felt more alone.

A good night's sleep supposedly makes everything better. I didn't have a good night's sleep but maybe it just being a new morning, another chance at a day, helps anyway.

We didn't really talk as we got up and dressed. We were leaving for breakfast, me heading out first, when Raf suddenly grabbed my arm and pulled me back in.

'I'm sorry, Noa. I'm sorry I…' His voice cracked. 'Well you know… You're the … my first. I'm sorry. [big pause] But this,' he gestured about wildly with his arms, 'us being all weird and distant and everything is crazy! I love you. I can't lose you.'

And I started crying – not the response I think he was looking for – and then I looked up and caught his eyes and we both looked so vulnerable and sad that I started laughing at how stupid we both were.

'I thought it was me,' I said. 'I thought you wouldn't want me anymore.' And then he mock strangled me and we agreed to take it slow for a while. He held me in this bear hug for just the longest time and then we only broke apart when my stomach did this embarrassing massive rumble and we realised we were about to miss breakfast.

Maybe we've been going about this all wrong. The plan's always been to rescue Jack and sneak all three of us back into the Territory. Oh yes, and we might also, somehow, as yet completely unplanned, bring down the whole regime. Hmmmmmm. But maybe the plan should be to go back and smuggle all the people we care about *out* of the Territory to live here in the Peak or other settlements like it.

Life here's kind and good. Take today. I was in the school again this morning. Cara and Elias were both no-shows which was a bit annoying as I was determined to find out more about them. Then in the afternoon I was on foraging duty with Raf and Ben. Ben showed us how to identify all these different types of edible seaweed and plants and how to dig for razor clams and set snares for rabbits. Raf was so interested in everything, it just made me love him a hundred times more. It wasn't enough for him to be able to do something, he had to understand it all, its evolution. Take the seaweed for example. He wouldn't just accept that we were just harvesting this one type of sea kelp but leaving the brown more bulbous one. He kept on saying how he'd read in *The Biology of Plants* that all types of seaweed that grew here were edible.

Ben laughed, he seems to spend his whole life cracking up, and said they knew because lots of people had tried it and it was really disgusting. They only ate it if supplies were properly low. I could tell Raf still wasn't convinced and I joined Ben in hysterics as Raf broke a piece off to try and then just couldn't make himself swallow it 'cos it was so vile. He face literally juddered, like he'd accidentally put a small rodent in his mouth along with the seaweed.

I guess it's this need to know for himself, to question

everything, that stopped him from uploading and becoming a freakoid so there is an upside to being massively anal.

This evening there was a group meeting that everyone had to attend. Me and Raf did exaggerated eye rolls at each other when we heard this. This was going to be LAME. I mean I've been to school council meetings and even a meeting for all the apartments in our block and they've always been the dullest, most petty things ever. Who's going to refill the water dispenser? Who's going to organise the mopping of the communal areas? What's going to be done about the late night noise from Flat 23?

This was different. This wasn't a bit dull.

OK, there was some sort of admin stuff to start with. Rotas to draw up. Reports on food stores. Reports on patients. I hadn't even realised there was anyone sick here. There are currently eleven people with malaria. They're kept separate at the western end of the Peak. Two died in the last week. That report was given by Cara and it was clear from how detailed it was that she's involved in their care, and this made me a bit angry to be fair. Giving her that much responsibility. Not to mention that the risks of getting malaria are surely much higher if you're spending loads of time next to someone with it. A mosquito doesn't exactly have to travel far after they've sucked it up from the sick person to then bite the person looking after them. So to put an eleven year old in charge, particularly an eleven year old who doesn't even realise the importance of mosquito repellent?? Maybe Cara and Elias have something wrong with them? Maybe their white hair means they've got some sort of wasting, ageing thing going on so they're seen as the people to sacrifice as their life expectancy is so low anyway? They don't seem weak though so it just doesn't add up.

Then a fire was lit and all I could think about were the flames and the heat and the light. There is something so magical about fire. You can totally see why wolves came to have a look and ended up as our dogs. People took it in turns to tell stories. And we just sort of stared into the flames, smelt the lavender of the mosquito repellent and let the words drift over us and weave us together.

That night, I snuggled into Raf's arms and asked him to tell me a story. He tried to wriggle out of it but I kept on asking with more and more exaggerated puppy eyes and finally he gave in to, 'stop your eyes popping out your sockets'. Hmmm. Maybe I hadn't looked as cute as I'd thought. And then he started this story. About a shark called Sam who was a vegetarian and was teased by all the other sharks for not catching and killing his own food. But then Sam swam off and befriended a massive whale that only ate plankton so was a vegetarian too. The whale came back with Sam and basically made all the other sharks realise what idiots they were and that you could be strong without destroying others.

'Isn't some plankton actually little animals?' I asked.

'Shut up, Noa Blake. That's not the point and you know it,' came the reply.

I fell asleep with a massive smile on my face.

I've been so tired by the evenings that I haven't spent that much time staring at the stars but I think, if I had, I would have seen them shift as everything seems to be aligning itself.

A trader came this afternoon.

One of the lookouts rang the bell during the afternoon work session. Three loud peals.

Raiders?

I was still on teaching duty so had to look brave in front of the kids even though all I wanted to do was run and hide. Maggie noticed my shaking limbs and came over.

'Raiders?' she literally laughed in my face. 'No, love. Three rings is for a trader. Raiders ... well there'd be much more noise, many more bells.'

But my heart was already a skip, hop and jumping. A trader was the one person who could help, who might have seen Jack.

I begged to be excused and raced out the Barn and

towards Annie's, figuring that an important person would most likely to be brought there first.

Annie looked up as I tore in. Casper, one of the other high-up guys glared at me, clearly wanting me to get out, but Annie smiled, touched his arm and asked me to come in. She got my impatience. My need.

The trader was an independent. All the traders that I'd heard about before were attached to settlements. They'd go out with some new knowledge or process to swap and then always return to the same place. Like a shuttle bus of knowledge. This guy worked on his own. The community life didn't suit everyone. He either came up with a new process on his own or foraged some properly good haul of useful stuff by himself and then went from settlement to settlement, trading it for food and shelter. This time he brought rosemary. Huge bundles of dried rosemary that he'd tied all over his upper body so he looked like a weird walking shrub. The smell filled the room and my mouth watered as I remembered the lamb with rosemary potatoes that mum used to make when I was a little kid. The rosemary adds to the potency of the mosquito oil, the trader explained. And pre-drying the rosemary increases the concentration of the active ingredient.

Annie looked impressed. No wonder, I suppose, if eleven of your people are sick with malaria. A deal was struck. One big bundle for four nights' food and shelter.

Finally it was my turn to speak.

'Have you seen a boy called Jack?' I asked, the words tumbling out of my mouth. I guess I deserved the *stupid girl, you expect me to work with that description?!!* look that he shot back. So I pulled myself together and described Jack in as much detail as I could until I got an *OK now that's too much information* look instead.

'Do you want to tell me his star sign too?' He let out a dirty, sarcy little laugh.

I felt all this animosity building towards this guy. How dare he sit there all smug and judge me? He doesn't know what I've been through. And then the trader opened his mouth again and I went from hating him to wanting to jump on him and kiss him, dirty little mouth and all.

He'd seen Jack.

Jack was alive.

Jack didn't have malaria, at least he didn't two days ago.

Jack was living in a settlement called the Fort a day and a half's walk to the south east.

I looked at Annie and didn't even need to get my question out. She didn't need to hear it to be able to answer.

'Yes,' she said. 'You're strong enough now. We will miss you and Raf, but you can leave tomorrow.'

Small and deadly.

A swarm of mosquitoes came in the night. We must have been dead to the world as I only woke when our mosquito net was shaking from side to side as millions of tiny wings brushed past. Ehhhhhhhhhhhhhhhhh. Their horrible cry. I shook Raf awake next to me and we just lay there, rigid, holding hands and praying that the net had no holes and that we'd put enough repellent on. And it felt so unnatural to just lie there. Your body wants to fight danger, or at least to flee from it. But you can't exactly fight a swarm of mosquitoes and if you get out of the net, you're way more likely to get bitten up.

I have no idea how long we stayed there. We waited till we couldn't see or hear any more of them and then waited a bit more after that just to make sure.

The first of the dawn light was cutting through the sky as we finally stumbled outside. On the street, all around, were other dazed people. Everyone was checking themselves. Had we been bitten? I felt all over my body, terrified that I'd find one. That they'd got me.

Nothing.

Nothing.

Nothing.

Then a bump. On my thigh. Oh God. I checked and

nearly choked on my relief at finding it was an ingrowing hair. Disgusting but in that split second I loved it. I could hardly bear to meet Raf's eyes in case he'd been got. He finished checking a few minutes after me and I don't think I took a single breath in all that time. Just as I was about to die from lack of oxygen, Raf announced, 'all clear', in a small, shaky voice.

Others weren't so lucky. Loads of the mosquito nets were really quite old now. They had holes that people'd tried to tape or sew up over the years, but it's so hard to make sure you've got every gap. And mosquito repellent might keep the odd mosquito away or even a small group, but it's not going to hold up against a swarm.

There was a meeting at the Barn. Everyone who'd been bitten had to stand on one side so we could count them. Twenty-seven. Including Ben and two of the kids from the school.

I heard someone cry out, 'No!' and it took a moment for me to realise that it'd been my voice. I think my brain was trying to go into a protective disconnect mode. For once Ben's face had no trace of a smile, like it wasn't him but a much more serious identical twin up there. Raf looked as upset as I felt.

More shelters were going to be turned into wards to observe and care for them, Annie continued, taking charge in her gentle yet authoritative way. Being bitten did not necessarily mean the person was going to get malaria or any other virus, she stressed. But, the strain of malaria the mosquitoes out here carried was a particularly nasty one. Symptoms normally appeared within twenty-four hours and within that time complications such as brain swell, liver failure and fluid-filled lungs were also common so anyone who'd ever done so much as a first-aid course was needed to help out.

She needn't have asked. Everyone helped. It's like a big family here. There was no talk of going back to sleep. There weren't prayers as such but as darkness started to fall, reed torches were lit at points all round the settlement, a bit like candles in a church. Annie confided that most settlements do it whenever something bad's happened or lots of people are sick. I guess religion doesn't have a monopoly on light as hope.

Flames don't just attract moths.

The Raiders came just before dawn. There was no warning as everyone, including the sentries, was involved in setting up the new wards, sponging down patients who'd already developed fever and re-darning mosquito nets. The sick bastards would have seen the burning reeds and known we were weak. Vulnerable to attack.

I don't know exactly how many Raiders there were.

Something in the region of fifteen to twenty. Their approach had been silent but once they'd come through the perimeter fence, their war cries tore the air like a hundred seagulls shrieking. They came armed with knives and club-like sticks and cut and kicked and hit their way from shack to shack. They had their faces smeared with mud, I guess as some sort of war paint or camouflage, but you could still see their features underneath. There were grown men, but there were also boys and girls not much older than me, eyes cold like stones, empty of empathy. How could they! I flung myself onto one of the girls' backs, but she threw me off and whacked her club into my stomach. I was doubled up on the floor, puking from the blow. Lying on the ground I could do nothing but watch. Watch as Raf was smashed against the wall by one of the bigger raiders; watch as Annie was pulled into the street with a knife to her throat; watch as the cow was dragged out of the settlement with no one daring to stop it in case that meant the death of their leader. Then came the worst bit. The Raiders' leader, this guy in his twenties with long dreadlocked blond hair, called for silence.

'No one else will be hurt,' his voice rang out, 'if you bring us your Cells.'

No one moved. Cells? I had no idea what he was talking about but it looked as if everyone else did. They seemed to shrink in on themselves a little as if to hide the secret in the folds of their skin.

'If you don't,' the Raiders' leader continued, 'this woman here will die.' There was a loud group intake of breath. The guy was clearly capable of killing. His clothes, if you could call his leather outfit that, was covered with dried and not so dried blood.

'Your Cells. NOW!'

'We have no Cells here,' Annie spoke, trying to keep her voice steady, but failing. She was speaking loudly. Speaking to all of us.

'Wrong answer,' the Raider shouted, and with that, to show his seriousness, he jabbed the point of his knife slightly into Annie's neck so a trickle of blood flowed down.

'You have one more chance before I gut your leader like a pig. Traders told us there are two of them here. But. (Pause followed by a crocodile's smile.) I'm in a generous mood. We'll just take the one. Give us the girl and we'll leave you in peace.' And he sort of snorted the word peace as if he'd just made this brilliant joke.

No one moved.

'You have thirty seconds.' Then the leader turned to this tall guy, lurking at the side. 'Ray, start torching the shacks.'

'Ray' walked forward, into the light so I got to see his face. Half of it melted like dripping wax. Oh God. Oh God, the psycho.

I'd like to say that I immediately sprang into action.

That I picked up something from the ground and took out Ray and then kept going, an unstoppable force, until every Raider, including the leader himself was gone too. I didn't. I squeezed my eyes shut like a toddler playing hide-and-seek as the leader starting counting and the buildings started burning.

Then, above all the chaos a voice cried out. 'Stop! Stop! I'll go with you if you just stop!'

I opened my eyes once more. Cara was walking towards the leader, oblivious to Annie's, 'Noooooooooo!'

The Raiders left with their prizes and we put out the fires. Looking around, the fire in everyone's eyes had been extinguished too.

And I finally found out what was so special about Cara and Elias. Maggie told me as I was helping her clear burnt timber out of the Barn, the secret no longer worth keeping. Some of the children who'd been born out here had been born with what must be some sort of genetic mutation. Their hair was white and their skin was whiter than normal, but that wasn't the important thing. They didn't get malaria.

And it wasn't just in the Peak. They'd heard talk about similar children at a number of other settlements. The few ex-scientists in the Peak have a theory that there's something different about the shape of their red blood cells meaning that the malarial plasmodium can't invade them.

'Like sickle cell anaemia?' I asked. We'd done this in biology.

'A bit like that but better. Sickle cell anaemia makes you weak and die young. These Cells, as they call them, aren't weak. They're the opposite. They're stronger than anyone. They're the only ones with a decent chance of survival.'

'But why do the Raiders want them?' I asked.

Maggie looked at me as if she didn't really want to answer and was clearly weighing up whether to make up something nice and reassuring or just tell me the truth. Like a parent when asked by a young kid about death.

She chose the truth. 'For breeding.'

Raf and I offered to delay our departure, said we'd wait until the Peak was on its feet again, but Annie insisted we left as planned. She said that we had to stick to our earlier decisions and not let our path be determined by THEM. She wouldn't say the word Raider. It hadn't left her lips once in the aftermath. Like she wasn't acknowledging them as people.

Annie presented us with a bundle and we both teared up a bit at her generosity. Inside were two flasks of water, some dried meat, salted cod and seaweed, a bottle of mosquito repellent oil and a tinderbox. We hugged her tightly, thanked her over and over and then turned to leave.

'One last thing, Noa,' Annie's voice followed me to the door.

'Yes?'

'Keep your humanity. It's your most precious gift. If you lose it, there is nothing left to fight for.'

I nodded and Raf gave my hand a little squeeze. We went round the settlement saying our goodbyes. I choked up a little as I hugged Maggie and we tried to talk to Ben but his fever was so high I'm not sure he even knew who we were. It was so hard leaving him, not knowing if he would make it. Knowing that the world would be a far poorer place if he didn't.

After pulling the strip of corrugated iron that served as the Peak's gate to, Raf took the compass from his backpack and we set off south east. The streams and pools were starting to get pretty deep so we often had to wind our way round, following the areas of higher land. Our legs were hurting by the afternoon but we kept on going, knowing the pain we were enduring was nothing compared to that of those we'd left behind.

We didn't talk much today. I think everything's just been a bit too much and silence can be cleansing. I mean, super religious monks and people just sit in silence all day and look twenty years younger than they actually are. I guess for us it was also that we didn't want to dwell on what had been and yet also it seemed wrong to get all happy and excited about seeing Jack again as if my happiness was the only thing that mattered. But maybe, I kept thinking anyway, if we could just get to Jack and get him back to the Territory we would have righted one wrong, one injustice and if everyone managed to do the same then we'd be some way towards making a mark. Making a dent in what was wrong with the world.

When it was too dark to continue safely, we made camp under some shrub bushes on a raised grassy mound. We decided against a fire as it wasn't that cold and we'd seen what flames could attract. I lay, wrapped up in Raf's arms. I was exhausted but I thought my brain and still-whirling thoughts would stop me sleeping. They did, but not for long. Soon the regular beat of Raf's heart and the warmth of his body soothed me into oblivion.

The day started so well. We reached the Fort before the sun was at the top of its daily arc. It was obvious, even from a distance, how the settlement had got its name. The hill it was on was of the high and pointy variety and the wet ground below surrounded it a bit like a moat. What's more, the fence that had been erected around the bottom was tall and spiky and topped with barbed wire.

Maybe they were on high alert for Raiders or something but a bell started clanging before we'd even had a chance to shout our hello.

We were met outside the fence by three of their guards/scouts – two guys and a girl, all not much older than us. One of the guys might even have been younger and he had that semi-feral look of the kids I'd taught back at the Peak, the ones who'd been born out here. I thought they might be going to turn us away, which would have made a real sick joke of our whole ordeal, everything we'd been through, but they didn't. They listened to what we had to say. At first one of the guys seemed to be saying they didn't know any Jack Munro and my heart plummeted straight through my chest into the ground below, sodden and salty. But then the girl piped up, 'Ryan, you know Jack – J – the big ginger guy, Megan's guy. The one who's ace at hunting.'

Raf snorted as if being 'ace at hunting' was the lamest thing ever, but that's just because he still hasn't managed to snare anything himself. But all I could hear were the words 'Megan's guy', and my heart shot back up into my chest and tore a new hole there. Jealousy was a new emotion to me. One that I hadn't anticipated. Not to do with Jack. At least not this way round. And it was the shock of it as much as anything that left my head reeling and my knees weak.

The three agreed to take us up into the Fort so we could see 'J' – (his name is Jack goddammit!) and talk to the Committee. Apparently everything in the Fort is decided by the Committee, elected once a year – they've rebelled against the Ministry by going into democracy overload.

I said that probably wasn't necessary as we were just going to take *Jack* and leave, but they laughed and said that we didn't really look like kidnappers so wasn't that up to *J*?

The girl scout/guard ran ahead so by the time we got to the main building, another converted barn – they called it 'The Meeting Room' 'cos they're up themselves – the Committee were already there looking pretty smug and self-important. There were ten of them, aged from about 15 to 25, all perched on a random assortment of salvaged metal chairs. They introduced themselves but I can't remember all their names. I heard 'Matt' and 'Frankie', but then I stopped listening because at that moment Jack walked in.

Jack.

I wasn't aware of any sort of thought process happening, but the next thing I knew, I was tearing across the floor and flinging myself up and around him. He held me there, off the floor, like I weighed no more than a bunch of sea-lavender. He'd healed. There were slight scars on his lower legs that emerged, freckled and triumphantly white – is he totally immune to tanning? – from a pair of dodgy brown shorts. His nose had this tiny kink in it, and he's lost some weight, but somehow in a good 'before' and 'after' photo shoot way as his muscles seem all the more prominent. But ultimately, there was little trace of the broken creature I'd last seen dragged into a cage by the Guards. This Jack was strong again. Tall again. Mine again.

'Jack!' was all I could manage to say. Just, 'Jack!' like a doll you press that makes one sound over and over.

He caught me up in a massive, bone-crushing bear hug and murmured, 'Noa!' into my hair.

Finally I got enough of a grip on myself to lean back and look him straight in the face.

'I told you I'd come and get you, didn't I?' I squeak-croaked, emotion turning my voice into that of a prepubescent boy.

'You could have gotten yourself killed, you denser,' he smiled back and I swear I saw his eyes begin to tear up.

He stroked my arms and looked startled as his fingers

traced the scar of the 'J' I'd carved there all those days ago. Jack's expression then changed to concerned with a little bit of pleased thrown in.

This is when it all went wrong.

One of the Committee members, this girl, Megan, pretty if you're into lithe girls with really thick brown hair and a beauty spot a.k.a. dirty face mole, stalked over, wrapped herself proprietorially round Jack's arm and stroked his more-obvious-than-before biceps.

I had no choice. I stepped back, nearly tripping over my feet as I withdrew. It was like a nature programme I once saw – *Recently Extinct Mammals* – where this lesser lioness had gone to all this trouble to catch an antelope and then had to surrender her prey to a more dominant cat.

Megan looked at me – up and down – taking in every flaw, every mark. Her eyes narrowed as she registered my arm.

'So…' her voice was barbed, 'you're the girl who ruined J's life.'

At that exact same moment, Jack clocked Raf standing in the middle of the room. I followed his gaze and Raf had that closed look on his face again. The one when he switches his eyes onto screensaver mode and I can't read him at all. Jack and I moved still further away from one another, our bodies stiffening. I thought we were both just embarrassed. Awkward. But with Jack it was more than that.

'What's the freakoid doing here?' His voice was ice.

Freakoid. The whole room fell silent and all eyes landed on Raf with the intensity of the search beams flanking the Fence.

Another Committee member, Adnan, stood up. 'You brought a freakoid here?!' Like it was the worse crime imaginable.

Two other girls from the Committee jumped forward, lifted up Raf's now shaggy mop of hair to reveal his Node. There was a collective sharp intake of breath. The air crackled.

'It's not like that.' I had to control the situation, could feel it about to turn nasty. 'He doesn't upload. He's one of us.' But they weren't listening.

'A freakoid could never be one of us,' another voice from the Committee, a girl's, Claire.

Have you forgotten how he treated you, Noa?' Jack's voice was now distilled anger.

'It was an act. It was to protect me.'

'What if it's just an act now?'

'We came to rescue you, you moron, quite why I'm not so sure now,' Raf spoke, his voice calm, too calm.

'I don't need your help. Do I look like I need your help?' Jack started to advance. Attack mode.

'He's here to spy on us,' Megan decreed. 'Somehow the Ministry knows. Maybe…' her voice fell to a whisper, 'Maybe they've got Simon.' Whoever Simon was, he was clearly massively important as this comment caused loads of scurrying and fearful whispering.

'Lock him up in Ward Three. That's empty,' Adnan ordered. So much for all decisions by committee.

'Her too,' from Megan.

Another bell rang and four big guys sprung forward and started to bundle us away. I was being pushed this way and that and my chest was hammering so hard in my chest it hurt to breathe.

'No, stop!' shouted Jack. 'Not Noa, she's not involved in this.'

'Quiet, babe,' replied Megan. 'You're not thinking clearly 'cos it's *her*. They're Ministry spies. No other reason for a freakoid to be out here. We should just stick a knife up his Node and be done with it.'

'No!' the scream tore from my throat.

'There'll be a trial.' Adnan seemed to have more authority than Megan. 'This is a place of democracy and fair trials. We're not going to sink to their level.'

We're now locked in a tiny room, our hands and feet bound. Our supplies gone.

Our trial is tomorrow.

This is not how it was supposed to go down.

I hate Megan and it appears that the feeling is mutual.

The trial was first thing after breakfast. Well, after everyone else's breakfast. We'd been given some dried meat last night but nothing since. Even that had stuck in my throat.

I didn't sleep at all last night. No, that's not quite right – I must have nodded off at one point as I can remember this terrible dream in which I was sinking slowly, ever so slowly, into this salt marsh and Jack was standing at the edge. He had longer arms than normal, ape-like arms that hung all the way to the ground but he wouldn't put them out, wouldn't even extend one the tiny bit needed to rescue me. Instead, he was explaining to me sadly that this was the only way to see if I was a spy. If I sank I was innocent. And I was all, 'But I'll drown,' but he just stood there nodding his head sadly. And then he somehow morphed into Megan and his right arm was now a long stick and was pushing me down, holding me under the water as the salt filled my lungs.

I must have called out and woken Raf as he was there as I came too, staring down blue and green comfort. I guess blue and green are the colours of the sea and Dad's got these old books about the power of the sea to de-stress. Before. Before it became associated with death and destruction that is. Raf curled his body round mine for the rest of the night, murmuring reassuring nothings into my ear. Telling me that we'd get through this. Telling me that the worst that could happen is that we'd be chucked out of the Fort, but then we'd make our way back to the Peak, stock up on supplies and get home. No one would even know we'd left. Jack was clearly fine and not some starving, damaged wreck, so in a way we'd achieved our mission. As a team we were invincible.

He didn't mention getting back through the Fence.

The Meeting Room had been cleared out and we were sat at a table facing the Committee. The rope round our feet had been cut so that we could walk there, but our hands were still bound and the skin round my wrists was red and sore where the rope cut into the flesh.

'Is this really necessary?' Raf had asked, but it just made them pull the rope tighter. 'For Simon,' the guard, this kid, had muttered as he pulled.

The trial was public so the space behind us was packed with the other settlers. I guess this was a more exciting than usual morning at The Fort. *What's it to be – water purification or watch two kids get lynched? Oh, the lynching please.* I craned my neck to try and see Jack but I couldn't make him out.

Adnan was Committee chair and sat in the middle. He called order and explained that we were here to be tried as Ministry spies attempting to infiltrate the Fort.

I wanted to stare at the floor, to block everything out, but I forced myself to look up, to stare the Committee members in the eye and challenge them to come to their senses.

'The penalty, if found guilty,' Adnan continued, 'is death.'

I froze, numb. Even the Ministry doesn't *directly* kill people. Raf was on his feet.

'This is crazy!'

'Be seated before the court.'

I hissed at Raf to sit down, knowing that pissing these guys off was not going to help us, and reluctantly he lowered himself down again, a muscle twitching in his jaw as he did so.

The 'prosecution' got to go first.

Megan moved from her seat to stand before the Committee. It was my turn to leap up too.

'If it please the court…' I was going for brave and TV show lawyery but my voice wavered in time with my shaking knees. 'It can't be fair for a member of the judging panel to also act as prosecutor.'

Megan opened her mouth but Adnan got in there first. 'Agreed.'

Megan opened her mouth again but Adnan silenced her with his hand.

'Megan will not participate in the judgement.'

Megan shot daggers at me then cleared her throat and started to speak. The picture she painted was horrific.

As everyone knew (apart from me and Raf clearly), Simon, her brother, (voice hushed at the mention of the golden one) was orchestrating a new wave of Opposition – the mobilisation of the Wetlands. A few carefully selected future leaders (she positively radiated smugness at this point so she must have been referring to herself) had been chosen to deliberately fail the TAA to be shipped out to the Wetlands. Here, they were to establish a settlement far from the prying eyes of the Ministry and collect all the people with the right skills, ultimately uniting the Wetlanders as an army.

Raf and I looked at each other. What?!!! We hadn't seen any evidence of this, heard no mention of it. Their plan clearly wasn't going massively well.

Now we turn up out of the blue – a freakoid and the daughter of a Laboratory employee (thanks for sharing Jack, after all – sharing is caring) under the transparent cover of a 'rescue' mission. Two *kids*. (She spat the word but she must be max three years older than us, and as Jack's my age, if we're such *kids*, that makes her a complete paedo.) 'Are we to believe that two amateurs with no training, no assistance somehow broke through the Fence undetected, somehow survived unharmed as they trekked across the Wetlands and are somehow in possession of mosquito repellent and tinderboxes that you can't just walk into a shop in the Territory to buy? Is it not more likely that the Ministry has somehow caught Simon, extracted a confession from him and is now using these … these (*contemptuous wave in our direction, like we didn't even deserve a noun*) to locate our centre of operations and destroy us?

After all, it was easy to see why we'd been selected as spies by the Ministry. Raf, being a freakoid, was a natural choice, his loyalty to the Territory would be absolute. I'd been coerced or bribed another way – maybe my services were in exchange for being allowed to 'pass' the TAA. (I wanted to punch her at this, punch the smug confidence off her moley face, but I forced myself to sit and chewed the inside of my cheek instead until I tasted blood.)

The Ministry knew that Jack, the son of a key old Opposition figure with his own violent streak – was likely to gravitate towards any settlement that might be planning an attack on the Territory. We would have been dropped deep into the Wetlands and left to figure the last bit out by ourselves.

We were Ministry stooges, with Ministry supplies, acting on information extracted by Ministry torture. As such we deserved to die.

By the time she finished the air was filled with boos and hisses and I thought we were going to be lynched then and there.

Now it was our turn.

I got to my feet and had to wait a few seconds for the room to stop spinning.

'You've got this all wrong. I, we, would never work for the Ministry.' My voice was quavering and no one was listening. The air was still buzzing with hate and no one was listening. This anger bubbled up inside and overflowed, drowning any residual fear.

'This is supposed to be a democracy. A fair trial. It's my time to speak now and you WILL listen!'

The room fell silent.

I explained that Jack's failing had been my fault and that I'd sworn to come after him. I detailed how we'd got here. How we'd clung to the underneath of a lorry, how we'd nearly died of dehydration, how we'd stayed at The Peak, all the things we'd witnessed there. I started flagging so Raf took over. He spoke about how he'd watched his sister change, how he'd sworn right from the start to never upload, how he hated the Ministry, how he'd thought of himself as strong but had never really known strength until he'd seen the resilience of the people at The Peak and how they not only survived, but fought for a good life, a better life, every single day.

The mood of the crowd had shifted, that was for sure, but had it shifted enough?

Adnan asked if anyone from the floor had relevant testimony. Silence … foot shuffling … silence…

'I do.' A voice clear and strong. Jack's voice. This could go either way.

'I can speak for Noa,' he said and Megan's face went all closed and angry cat.

'Noa's a good person. She would never, ever, act as a Ministry spy. It doesn't surprise me in the least that she managed to beat all the odds to get here. She made a promise to me that she'd come and she's so stubborn that there's no way that she'd let anything stop her.' There it was, short and sweet. Jack wasn't much of a large group talker, didn't naturally have a way with words, but when he spoke people listened, and they were listening now.

'But what about the freakoid,' shouted a voice from the crowd. 'Why's he here?'

'Because he's in love with her,' Jack answered flatly. 'People do crazy things when they're in love with Noa Blake.' He turned to sit back down in the crowd. He hadn't looked at me once.

'But,' Megan was on her feet again, trying to rile the crowd up again, trying to get people back on her side, 'do you really believe a promise and guilt is motivation enough to risk everything to come here? If she really is no spy, then Noa has not only put her own life at risk but she has also jeopardised the lives of her parents if she's caught. Would she really do that because of a promise? Would anyone do that? Ask yourselves, is there another explanation? Why has she really come?'

Now it was Raf's turn. I could hardly keep track. People were bobbing up and down. We hadn't been given breakfast. My blood sugar levels were plummeting. Raf's words brought me back from the edge. Brought everything very much back in focus.

'Because she's in love with Jack, even if she doesn't realise it herself.'

I wish I may, I wish I might, have the wish I wish tonight.

As I was heading for bed a huge shooting star burnt its way to the ground. It seemed like it was really close, just a few kilometres away or something, but I guess it was probably more like thousands of miles. I closed my eyes and wished, wished like I had when I was a little girl sat on her mum's knee who still believed in magic and Father Christmas and the power of kisses to heal wounds. Then I used to wish for a huge range of stuff. That sea levels would stop rising. That Uncle Pete would cancel his visit. That Rex wasn't dead.

Tonight I wished that things would be less horrifically awkward between me and Raf and Jack. I guess that wish has about the same probability of coming true.

We won the trial. The Committee found us not guilty of spying by seven to two. So we're free to go – or stay –

as long as we 'prove useful', which seems to translate into help with chores and stuff or train as part of the new wave of super fighters. I mean, *really*. They also want to 'compare our plans to breach the Fence'. Steal ours more like. There was something a bit desperate about the way they asked. Not sure how they'll react when they find out we've got no plan as yet. I don't think 'wing it' really counts.

I thought Raf would want to pack up and head off immediately but he's said we'll wait. He double-checked the day count on the arm of his backpack. If we're not to be missed, we need to be back in the Territory in eleven days. That gives us some leeway. So I've got three days to 'work out what I want'. I mimed incomprehension but he smiled. It was a flinty smile, all mouth, no eyes.

'You know what I mean, Noa. Three days.'

That's about the sum of the conversation we've had since the trial. He's sleeping in a guys' dorm, leaving me to share with Megan, Tara and Alice. Everyone's thrilled about that arrangement. I was worried that they might try and off me in my sleep so I attempted to doze with one eye open. It's impossible. Instead, I slept lightly and fitfully.

I saw Raf at breakfast when chores were divvied out. Even amazing armies that no one's heard of need fresh water, food and mosquito repellent. Raf got water purification, as did ten other people, which seemed crazy.

At the Peak it was a job for max two or three people so I don't know if 'water purification' is code for some super-special-need-to-know work or something. I tried to give Raf a 'what?!' look but he just stared back, all blank and expressionless.

I got mosquito repellent which I was quite pleased about until the task was subdivided and I didn't get the fun prance-about-in-purple-fragrant-fields bit. I got the peel-yellow-fat-off-dead-animals-and-boil-it-up-in-a-big-pot bit. I suggested that maybe I should help at the school instead as I'd had loads of practice at that. That got me laughed at.

'There's no school here. This is a training camp for war.'

They're so up themselves. Chores were over at lunchtime and then we had to train. How sprints and squat jumps are going to give me anything other than blisters and sore thighs is beyond me. They act like this is a massively important command centre and they're so paranoid about spies. But no one even mentioned them at the Peak so if their war cry hasn't spread to pretty nearby settlements then I really don't think the Ministry is really going to be too fussed. Jack even said that he just stumbled across this place, dehydrated and starving. It's not like he'd heard about it and wanted to be some crazy warrior. Well, not then anyway.

I managed to speak to Jack just before sun down, having finally got him to myself away from Raf's judging eyes and Megan's claws. It didn't go so well. Nothing's going so well right now.

He stood away from me. Like he didn't trust himself to touch me. Or maybe he just didn't want to.

'I'm not coming back with you, Noa.' There was no trace of doubt in his voice.

'But you can't stay here. You'll get malaria – even with the repellent – no one can survive loads of mosquito swarms.'

'So I come back and hide in your closet?'

'It won't be like that.'

'But it would. Suppose we make it through the Fence. I'm then living in a place where I don't officially exist. I can't work. I won't have a ration card. And every second of every minute of every hour of every day I'll know that any moment, any time, I can be stopped by a policeman and be right back here again. Or shot. I'm not sure the Ministry is that into second chances. And what about all the other Norms in the Territory? The ones who'll fail and get shipped out here? The ones who get experimented on?'

My shock must have registered on my face. I'd never told Jack about what Mum did. What she had to do.

'Megan told me. The Opposition found out a few years ago. It's one of the reasons she volunteered to fail on purpose.'

I swallowed. This was making me feel worse and worse. I preferred the Megan I'd put in the box of evil, manipulative, boy-stealing bitch. That way it was easy to hate her.

'So do we just forget about them? The Ellas of this world. The kids who don't have a chance? Don't know them. Don't care. Is that it?'

I didn't know what to say so I said nothing. It was horrible hearing it spelt out so bluntly.

'No, I'm staying here, Noa. We're doing something important here. We're taking action.'

'Yeah, I can see that.' I wanted to bite back the words as soon as they'd left my mouth.

Jack's eyes hardened.

'Megan was right about you. All you care about is yourself.' His right fist started pulsing and this muscle in his face was twitching.

'You didn't come here for me. You came here for you. To rescue your *plaything*. Your back up in case you tire of Raf. You don't want me to be with anyone else just in case you change your mind.'

'No! That's not it at all.'

'Then choose me.' Jack's voice was suddenly soft and vulnerable, all the anger evaporated. 'Come with me right now and stand next to me as you tell Raf and tell Megan and tell all the others that you choose *me*.'

I tried to speak but my mouth just opened and closed like a denser goldfish.

'As I thought.'

And he was right, in a way. In the dark of night, lying on my salvaged mattress bed, looking deep into my selfish heart, I know he was right. I'm not sure that it is him that I want. I love him, I know that now, but maybe in too comfortable a way. Like we've leapfrogged the whole fireworks stage and are an old married couple. Raf is fireworks. But still the thought of Jack with someone else kills me.

Choose me or lose me. Or mess about deciding, be slow to choose and lose both anyway.

I think I've truly messed things up this time. So much for having three days to decide. It's been one day and Raf's drawing further and further away from me. He's gone from being a virtual leper – *freakoid, freakoid* – to settler of the month. Like he's got some special popularity gravity that's sucking all approval towards him, leaving me empty and alone.

'Water purification' wasn't a special-secret-need-to-know code word. It was just water purification. Done badly. Raf noticed that they were using the tarp and water trough design but had forgotten/never learnt the add a big stone in the middle part so loads of the pure water that was condensing was falling back into the salt pool instead of into the collecting container. This meant they were producing a tiny fraction of the pure water they should have been. All Raf did was add the stone and now people are talking about him like he's this scientist extraordinaire – freeing up more people and time for 'training'. Adnan slapped him on the back this morning and even Megan, who'd wanted to stick a knife down his Node twenty-four hours ago, smiled at him at breakfast.

This 'genius' on his part has also meant that the Committee are now taking us, or rather him, seriously as players in the fight against the Ministry. Tonight we're having our big meeting comparing notes on breaking through the Fence and we get to hear their plans for ultimate revolution. I think they might be planning to recruit Raf to some important position. Me – well I'm sure there's more fat to boil.

Luckily out here there's never that much time to dwell on things. There's always some task to do. Survival's good like that. I was on seaweed collection today, which was fine. Lots of trekking, identifying, cutting, washing, boiling and iodine extraction but it wasn't too arduous. And I got to build a fire. Lee showed me how. He's on the Committee so when he first rocked up to train me and a couple of other relative newbies I thought Oh No! But he's actually pretty cool. Dark, almond-shaped eyes, a shock of black hair, a serious face but with a smile that breaks though as suddenly as a seagull attack. He seemed wary of me at first but then thawed. His story is pretty amazing too. He's difficult to age but definitely a couple of years older so I asked if he'd volunteered to fail as well. But he said no, that was a new thing. He predated that. He'd failed 'cos he'd had points deducted.

'I had a point deducted too. It was so unfair!' We were properly bonding. Me and the cool older guy were actually pretty similar. Someone else in the group snort-laughed and I didn't know why. It was clearly an at-me rather than with-me laugh.

'What?!'

'Tell her.'

'No. It's not important.'

'Lee had twenty points deducted. For hacking the school computer network.'

'Oh.' Rather less similar than I'd first imagined.

I worked pretty much in silence after that for a while. But then Lee made a point of coming up to me at the end.

'You did good today.'

I needed the praise. It seemed like ages since someone had said anything half nice to me and I soaked it up like a dehydrated plant.

'And don't worry too much about Megan. She's not as harsh as she seems.'

I raised an eyebrow.

'She's just passionate, that's all. You should have seen her when she first came to The Fort. She and Adnan. To recruit us. We were just getting by. Learning how to forage, getting information from traders. It was a smallish settlement as we're pretty far from the drop zone. She whirlwinded in and told us about their plan to create an army of Wetlanders and you just couldn't help but go with it. To follow the flame. That's what she does to people. But she'll do anything for others as well, mind you. You know Lotte?'

I shook my head as a fleeting glimpse of fear showed on his face.

'What?'

'Nothing. It's probably fine. You'll know soon enough… Megan practically adopted Lotte when her parents died two years ago, back when people here hadn't heard of … well, they kind of shunned her. And Jack – well you've seen first hand how much she likes him! There's only been one other person out here I've seen who's quite so single mindedly … well, let's call it *determined*.'

'Who's that then?'

'You, Noa, you – you should have seen yourself at the trial. Adnan noticed it too. Megan mark 2.'

Something strange happened on the way to the meeting. No, that's not quite right. Two strange things happened on the way to the meeting. First, I saw Megan laugh. As in belly laugh, all natural with no malice in sight. She was walking along, sweaty from training and hand in hand with a girl of about twelve, who looked up at Megan adoringly as if she were the source of life itself and all its secrets. And Megan looked down at her the way I've caught Mum looking at me, especially when she thinks I'm not looking, all fierce protective love. There was clearly this super special bond between them and – the girl was a Cell. She must have been – she had the telltale pale skin and white hair and weird glow – no you can't really call it a glow as there was no trace of pink to her cheeks – luminosity is a better word – of health. She must have been Lotte, the girl Lee was talking about and it explains why he'd gone all weird for a moment when mentioning her.

That moment decided something for me. It's like it took my heart, shook it, and gently realigned the pieces slightly. It's the moment I let Jack go. Megan isn't some witch. She might hate me and I was never exactly going to be best friends with the girl who tried to lynch me, but I felt like I saw into her soul in that split second and her soul was good. She wanted Jack. She would care for him, love him. I had to let her have him. Let him choose happiness even if it meant drawing a line in permanent marker through my life. I couldn't sit on the fence forever. Some fences were electric.

I reached over and took Raf's hand as he walked next to me. And squeezed it.

He turned, slowly, to look at me.

His eyebrows asked the question and my pitifully open face gave the answer. I'm yours if you still want me.

'I don't need three days,' emotion croaked out the words and luckily Raf scooped me up in his arms so he didn't have to see my tear-soaked face.

The meeting was a small affair, but you could almost smell its seriousness as you walked into the room, somewhere underneath the distinctive animal fat/lavender combo. All the Committee members were already there in the Meeting Room, sat in a circle on the floor. Everyone equal, no one at the head. It was admirable, but also kind of nauseating. As me and Raf entered, they all looked over and the circle broke to include us. Adnan smiled his welcome, Lee went from super serious to grinning in a heartbeat (maybe he's schizophrenic) and Megan made some sort of grimace that could have been a smile or maybe just a sneer. Sat next to Megan and avoiding eye contact was Jack. He must have been promoted to the inner circle. Jack saw me holding Raf's hand and did a weird little headshake.

Adnan spoke first.

'The purpose of today's meeting is to pool information and resources in order to better defeat our common enemy.'

Lots of wise nods. Maybe sage is a better word. Sage nods.

'In particular, to compare plans to breach the Fence.'

This caused a hush of expectation and everyone, me included, seemed to hold their breath for a beat at the possibility that someone might have a plan – someone might know how to achieve the impossible.

Then there was this burst of machine gun chatter as every stupid and implausible solution was spat out at once: 'Dig... Cut ... Climb... Pole vault.' Honest to God, some denser actually said pole vault. Like we were going to invade a school sports day or something.

'Quiet!'

It was Lee's voice this time, and pretty effective it was too, as the room returned to this expectant hush.

'I think there are some preliminaries we should discuss first.' He turned to me and Raf. 'What exactly were you planning to do?'

Hmmmm. Good question. Raf wasn't saying anything so I opened my mouth.

'It's quite simple really,' (nervous sarcastic laugh), 'we were going to find Jack and then the three of us were going to get back through the Fence together, before anyone realised we were missing, and keep Jack hidden in the Territory.'

Saying it out loud made it seem the densest plan ever and the looks we got suggested that everyone agreed.

'So no revolution? No overthrowal?'

I shook my head.

Megan bark laughed.

'Look we wanted to save Jack. But any more, well … you know what they do to the families of Opposition members.'

'What they do to all poorer families anyway – tear them apart. And do you really think that hiding Jack isn't an act of opposition? Do you really think that you're not already planning to put your parents in loads of danger anyway? You're just scared, to take the next step that's all,' and maybe it was just the exhaustion catching up with me or maybe it was Megan's ghost of a smugish smile, but whatever it was it really pushed my buttons.

'So what you've got planned is loads better, is it? An army of Wetlanders. Suppose you breach the Fence somehow, then what? You've got about 100 recruits as far as I can tell and there aren't exactly lots more flocking to join you every day. Maybe three or five people could sneak through undetected but an 'army' – no way. You'll be mown down. Every last one of you will be killed. Everyone you love – Jack, *Lotte*, all of them, gone.' Megan's eyes flashed as I mentioned Lotte's name. She clearly didn't know I knew about her. 'And then the Ministry will think that Fish are potentially dangerous, annoying at best, so they decide not to make anymore. They won't ship people out who fail, they'll just kill them. And they'll probably bomb all the settlements out here as well. All the good people, the kind people we met at the Peak, the independent traders, the Cells they'll be ripped apart – for what? For nothing!'

'We're considering different options.' Adnan's voice was on ultra-calm mode. 'We might go for an elite advance party followed by a more general invasion.'

'A team of assassins,' chimed in Frankie, face like a pick axe, who sat to Adnan's left. 'To destroy Womb Pod facilities and stop any freakoids from being born.' She was getting worked up as she spoke and tiny bits of spittle flecked the edges of her mouth. 'Wipe out the freakoids and at least the system is fairer.' She looked round the room and seemed to register Raf's presence for the first time. Her eyes went to the floor, guiltily. 'No offence, Raf.'

'None taken,' said Raf wryly. 'I can see why it's better to be on the side of the baby killers.'

'OK,' Megan entered the fray. 'We're not all in agreement about the Womb Pods.' She shot Frankie a look of disgust. 'But freakoids. We have to end the freakoid programme. Think about it, they're all passing, every year, so the proportion in the population is growing and growing. They'll be the majority. A majority of unfeeling robots with ultimate belief in and obedience to the Ministry. There'll be no one left to protect the weak, to protect our humanity.' In that moment she reminded me of Annie – well a far more feisty and bitchy version.

'You're forgetting something,' I couldn't let them keep going, they needed to understand. 'Freakoids are victims too. Lots of angry eyes and 'yeah, rights' were hurled in my direction. This wouldn't be easy.

'They didn't choose to have the procedure. It was done before they were born, or even if they got a late upgrade do you think they genuinely *chose* it?' I thought of Daisy and nearly choked up. But this wasn't a time for crying. 'Of course not, it was their parents' choice. And the whole personality thing – that's not the kid itself. That's the uploads. Look at Raf. He didn't upload – he's totally normal. No psycho tendencies at all. Remember any freakoid kids you used to play with before they uploaded?' No one was nodding. No one got it. I guess they hadn't been to a school like Hollets, hadn't seen how freakoids changed. I was beginning to despair when Lee backed me up.

'She's right you know. I knew a freakoid kid, Thom, when I was little. Totally normal guy, a good mate actually. Until he was ten. Until he began to upload.'

'So you're saying it's not the freakoids we need to destroy,' Adnan concluded. 'It's the uploads.'

And there it was. I think that's the exact moment Raf

and I joined the Opposition. Sorry, Mum. Sorry, Dad. I feel a little sick at putting you in danger, but Megan was right in a way. I put you in danger the moment I climbed under that truck. And we have to do this. You raised me to do what's right and this is right. I don't think we're coming home after all.

When I was about eleven I'd been ill for quite a long time, some virus or other, and felt totally drained. Mum got me these specially potent vitamins to help 'build me up again'. They were bright orange and you dropped them in a glass of water so they fizzed up and then you drank it all down. Afterwards I'd get this really intense surge of energy like my batteries had been recharged and then some. This is what I felt like when I woke this morning. Buzzing. High on life. Part of something epic – an 'elite team'.

Last night's meeting ended with the 'elite team' being picked: Me, Raf, Megan, Lee and Jack. We're supposed to have 'complementary skills'. Megan's seen as a feisty leader and was one of the founders of the Opposition out here so she was always going to be at the forefront of any attack or reconnaissance. Lee's hacking skills are going to be essential if we're to hack into the Ministry Servers to access and change the uploads. Jack was Megan's choice and is going to be invaluable if we need any brute strength. Me and Raf have apparently shown ourselves to be 'resourceful' as we managed to break through the Fence in one direction at least. I was surprised Adnan wasn't coming too but I guess someone needed to look after the Fort in our absence. Megan was torn between taking Lotte and leaving her behind but decided in the end that she'd be safer staying put. Our chances of success weren't the choicest.

When something gets decided out here, there's no sitting around. Our bags are packed. We have water, dried meats and seaweed and mosquito repellent. Today we hiked a couple of hours from camp in the direction of the Fence for advanced spy training. Megan led us. This place is one of their normal training camps. So there's a hut, equipment and a spade. A spade instead of a toilet. This is what my life has come down to.

I was quite into Robin Hood as a kid. Jack and I would play it sometimes. Daisy would be Maid Marian, I'd be Robin and Jack would be Will Scarlett. We'd pretend gallop around, pretend fire arrows left, right and centre and pretend distribute sacks of gold and food to our pretend adoring fans. There are no bows out here – it seems it's pretty tricky to carve one that actually fires an arrow in the direction you want it to go. There are slingshots, though, and I'm a pretty ace shot. Raf too. Jack and Lee less so. They both managed to shoot off a stone at incredible speed but at nearly a compass point in the wrong direction. It got so bad that I started to flinch every time one of them fired. We had to practise by piling up a pyramid of small stones, putting a target like a different coloured stone or twig on top and then stepping back five/ten/twenty paces and firing. Megan said it worked best if you cleared your mind. Went all Zen like these warriors used to do in ancient Japan. That way you became 'one' with the slingshot and were more likely to aim right as your subconscious mind takes over and for some reason that seems to be particularly good at judging how best to knock over a white pebble. We tried to find some rabbits or birds to practise on as it's harder to hit a moving target but there were none around.

We then moved onto knife practice. Megan gave us each a weapon and demonstrated throwing and stabbing techniques. She'd got these straw stuffed bags out from the hut and these were 'the enemy'. I managed to deal some pretty nasty blows to my straw foe when Megan announced we were moving up a level. She brought out another round of stuffed bags but someone had put some work into these. There were crude faces, etched on with charcoal, straw for hair, and basic clothes. They were nothing like people really but even so, I couldn't attack them in the same way. My arm lost its steel and my stabs turned half-hearted.

I think I'm going to stick with slingshot as weapon of

choice as the idea of actually piercing flesh, slicing a human like cutting up an apple just makes me want to puke. Crushing with a stone seems somehow better. Messed-up logic, I know.

I also know, or at least am supposed to know, how to disable an attacker silently. If they're running at you, you wait until they're three metres away, three metres is key, then move forward. You kind of grab their arm, swing your body round their back and then bring your other arm up round their throat so you have them in a chokehold. Keep applying pressure for long enough and they'll suffocate. As a final flourish you can also twist their neck so it breaks. And the puke feeling's back.

We partnered up. Me and Raf were together. He ran at me and I tried to swing round him but I mistimed it and moved too soon. I ended up hanging off his back as if he was giving me a piggyback. Then he turned me upside down and started tickling me and I couldn't stop laughing.

Until Megan's voice yelling in my ear suddenly meant it wasn't quite as funny any more.

'Sorry, is this a joke to you? Some sort of hilarious adventure?'

I was silent. I felt like such a denser.

'This is real. People will attack us. If you can't defend yourself you will be killed. If you can't silence someone, the whole team's safety is at stake. Come here. Now run at me… Faster!'

I sprinted towards Megan and in seconds she was wrapped round my body and I couldn't breathe. Blood was pounding in my ears and my eyesight was going all pixilated and my chest felt like it was going to explode. Then she released her grip. I gasped for air and rubbed my bruised ribs.

'See. That's how you do it. Now try again.' Everyone practised in silence. It seemed more real now. We kept swapping partners so you got to see how to change your stance, your swing to fit different-sized assailants. The three-metre rule stayed fixed though.

Raf versus Jack was pretty intense. Jack caught Raf in a stranglehold and looked like he'd never let go. It was like a weirdly physical embrace and the energy between them was crackling, almost like they were a bit gay. They'd better not be gay. That would be just my luck! Raf's eyes were bulging and his lips were starting to go blue when I looked over and gave a yell of, 'Jack!!!!' Megan turned to see and break it up. I didn't hear what she was saying but she was clearly mad. I just caught the end, 'Sort it out or be replaced.' I actually respected her a bit as she was obviously mad with Jack too.

As we camped down for the night, Lee ran through our tentative plan. He'd sketched the outline at the end of our meeting last night – the brilliant Fence scaling reveal – but now was the time for the detail.

'We hike due west as that's the most direct route to the Fence. Now the electricity for the whole Fence can't be supplied by just one circuit – it must be split into smaller sections, multiple circuits.' Of course, that made sense. 'All we need is for one circuit – the one supplying the section of the Fence we're at – to be down. Then we can get across. Cut, climb, whatever. There'll be a way.'

'What about the machine-gun towers?' Raf asked.

'We think they're automated too. Hopefully on the same circuit.' I nodded. That's what I'd thought. I described what I'd seen happen to the mother and child.

'How do we disable a circuit?' Jack looked dubious. This all seemed a bit too much like Physics for his liking. To be fair it was for me too. I get school level Physics – electricity is energy, making it destroyed our planet, if you stick a screwdriver in a plug socket you'll fry. But real world electricity. Hmmm. Bit beyond me.

Lee took over again. This part of the operation had clearly been his brainchild. 'All important circuitry is regularly tested to ensure it's functioning properly. The Fence is about as important as it gets so stands to reason there'll be regular checks – intervals when each individual circuit is turned off for a very short period. We have to work out the pattern and be ready.'

'So we get to the Fence and then watch and wait?' Jack asked.

'That's about it,' replied Lee.

Raf wasn't going to be left out. 'But how can you see if a circuit's down?'

146

'We'll keep sending test objects at it.'

So we sit, watch and what – throw small animals at the Fence until they stop frying? This was not sounding brilliant.

'And, assuming we get through,' I added, trying to focus on our mission beyond the Fence, 'where are the Ministry Servers?'

I thought Megan would answer. After all it was her brother who was high up in the Opposition and weren't they supposed to know this sort of thing? The location of key targets. If this was war, wasn't rule number one 'know your enemy' or at least know where your enemy keeps important stuff? But Megan said nothing and neither did anyone else. There was just stony silence and a couple of swallows.

No one knew.

It typically goes like this – a little kid is scared of the dark. They think there's something or someone evil lurking out there: in their cupboard, under their bed, outside their house. Their parents tell them that they're OK and there's nothing to fear. Except often there is. Little kids are right. Bad stuff happens in the dark.

This time we didn't get to see the bad stuff – just the aftermath. Jack was awake first and his horrified cry woke the rest of us in seconds. From due east a huge dark grey plume of smoke rose towards the sky, licking the clouds.

The Fort was on fire.

No one had to take charge for us to know what to do. Clothes were flung on, everything else was jammed back into bags and we were off, sprint-walking towards the smoke. The final approach we took more slowly, running from gorse bush to gorse bush in an attempt to hide our presence. In case the fire wasn't an accident. In case of attack. It wasn't the greatest attempt at concealment as it's pretty hard to squeeze five people behind a bush, they're just not big enough. And it's hard to creep silently between them when you're sending up sizeable splashes of water. Anyway, we needn't have bothered. When we eventually got to the perimeter fence, a section had been torn open like the top of a tin can and the attackers – it was now clear that this was nothing accidental – had been and gone.

We got halfway up the main path through the Fort before we saw anyone. Then Frankie came staggering out of a nearby shack. The shack was made of corrugated iron sheets so had survived the blaze. Frankie's clothes were ripped and the left hand side of her face bloodied. She seemed dazed and wasn't speaking. Megan grabbed her and I was afraid she was going to try and shake some sort of information out of her but instead she hugged her, sat her down and stroked her hair.

'What happened here, Frankie? Was it … the Ministry?'

Frankie took a deep gulp of air and finally spoke, her voice a hoarse croak as if something had happened to her windpipe.

'Raiders,' was all she managed.

Raf and me looked at one another in horror. Did these sick guys never stop?

'How did they get through? Didn't anyone sound the alarm? Who was on duty?' Lee's voice wasn't soft. It was urgent, harsh, and allowed no interval in which to answer his onslaught of questions.

'Fred was on duty but he didn't spot them in time. Maybe they were camouflaged, maybe he fell asleep.'

'We need to question him, where is he?' Lee again.

'Dead … they cut his throat.'

An awful thought came to me. An echo of past horrors.

'Why did they torch the buildings?' I asked, trying to keep my voice neutral and calm.

Frankie's eyes welled up with tears. She didn't want to answer.

Megan tried again, 'Frankie love, I know this is really hard for you, but why did they torch the buildings?'

'So Adnan would tell them.' The sobs were getting louder, wracking her body.

'Tell them what, Frankie?'

Frankie wouldn't answer. She wouldn't look Megan in the eye and instead started picking at bits of ash on the ground, turning her fingers grey.

Images of Cara kept flashing into my head. A slide show of Cara and the leader of the Raiders and the guy with half a melted face.

'Did they want Lotte?' I asked in a whisper. No reply – just louder sobs so I gently used my right hand to cup her chin and turn her face towards mine. 'Frankie, is that it? Did they want Lotte?'

Frankie met my gaze and nodded and Megan gave out this awful cry – primal – grief as a sound. Her softness and patience was gone.

'Did he give her to them? Did he hand over Lotte?'

'He had no choice, Megan. They'd finished burning the wooden buildings. They'd heard we had a Cell and they said they were going to start killing everyone here if he didn't hand it over.'

''The Cell?!? IT?!? Lotte's not a thing. She's a person. A *little girl*. You're trained fighters. I'VE trained you as FIGHTERS,' Megan spat out the words in disgust. 'So why didn't you FIGHT?!'

'It was the middle of the night. They had weapons. We weren't … prepared.'

But I don't think Megan heard her answer. She'd already broken. It was a sight I hadn't thought I'd see. Megan curled into a ball crying and Jack comforting her, his body fitting perfectly round hers, encapsulating her, insulating her from her pain.

Raf nudged me to leave and we slunk off, didn't want

to intrude on something so private. With Lee's help we tracked down Adnan and began to help others clear the debris and ash that blanketed the ground like dirty snow. Grey-white flakes decorated the door frames and dusted hair and eyebrows. It was almost beautiful.

We didn't get to do too much to help in the end. Adnan seemed to have things pretty much under control. The fire was now out and the smoke more of a dragon's puff than a full-on volcano. Adnan called a Committee meeting and wanted 'the team' to set out again immediately. To continue our mission against the 'tyranny of the Ministry'. Lee voiced his agreement, but something didn't feel right. I nudged Raf so he turned to look at me and I caught the same unease in his eyes. We'd done this before. Walked away before. How many times would we walk away?

'I'm going after Lotte,' Megan's voice was flat.

'Think about the mission,' Adnan was trying to sound caring but his impatience shone through, 'the life of one is nothing compared to the lives of thousands, the hundreds of thousands that are being destroyed by the Ministry. You know that more than anyone. That's why we're here. We can't lose focus.'

'I'm still going after Lotte.' All Adnan had done was add sparks to Megan's eyes.

'I'll come with you.' Jack squeezed her hand as he spoke. Ever-dependable Jack.

'This is crazy,' Lee added. 'Come on, guys. We need to remember who the enemy is here.'

'Maybe there's more than one enemy.' All eyes turned to Raf. 'The Raiders took Cara, a young girl from the Peak. They've now taken Lotte. Who knows how many more they've taken. They terrorise the settlements and even stop some from trading altogether. If we base decisions on numbers and start of think of people as statistics rather than actual human beings then we're no better than the Ministry. We need to remember that every person counts. Every life counts. I vote we bring the fight to the Raiders. We can't stop the seas rising, we can't stop the mosquitoes swarming but we CAN rescue Cara and Lotte and any other Cell they've captured and make the Wetlands a safer place.'

There should have been stirring music accompanying this speech, but anyway, even with just a backdrop of smoke and seagull caws I still felt swept up by Raf's words and felt pretty damn proud of my rebel-rousing boyfriend. I sat there with a stupid grin on my face until I realised some sort of response was expected from me.

'I'm with you.' And then I was back to the stupid grin again.

Megan and Jack stared at us in surprise and Megan even reached over and gave me and Raf a quick hug.

'Lee?' Adnan's voice was now resigned.

'Well, I guess I'm in too.'

And that was that.

Adnan allocated another ten people to our team. They were to return to base with the rescued prisoners and we'd press on to the Fence. If all went well. I didn't like to think quite how big that IF was.

So we were now fifteen against God knows how many. But we had an advantage. They didn't know we were coming for them.

The Raiders had left to the north-west and had a three-hour head start on us. We knew we had to hurry if we were to stand any chance of catching up with them, of following them and finding their base. They'd taken the Fort's pair of sheep as well as Lotte so they wouldn't be running or anything. They'd probably be tired as well – they'd have been marching all night. Attacking and ravaging probably takes it out of you a bit.

They'd been spotted starting out along this raised ridge of land so this was our setting off-point. The ridge continued for a couple of miles, so this set our course as it made sense that the Raiders would have stuck to it – after all, walking on dry land certainly beats wading. We marched to the end, trying to ignore the weight of my backpack digging into my shoulders, the constant ache in my knees – three days' supply of water isn't light. I wanted to stop, to sit and rest, but I knew if I ever let myself relax I'd never be able to stand up again.

Then it was decision time. There were two obviously drier routes. One would skirt another settlement, one would go across empty marshland. We chose the second. We figured the Raiders would have their hands full and wouldn't want to risk a potentially hostile encounter. It also made sense that their base was slightly removed. After a quick water break, we were off again, marching along the path through the marsh.

The Raiders were still not within sight, and as the land was pretty flat apart from a distant woodland and an even further hill, this meant that they were a considerable distance ahead of us. Daylight started to fade and my feet were beginning to blister up badly but we kept marching, kept to the raised drier route, hoping that we'd chosen the right way.

As the sun properly set we reached the wood. Well, what used to be a wood. Skeletal trees clawed at the sky, their branches completely bare of leaves. The salt must have killed them but left their root structure intact so they still stood there. A tree graveyard. It felt so unnatural that

I shivered. I think everyone was a bit creeped out as we were all talking about it when Raf suddenly hissed, 'Quiet'. He signalled to deeper within the forest. I squinted, saw nothing, squinted again and then registered what he'd seen. A fire. Nothing major like at the Fort. Nothing out of control. A nice contained campfire. Lit by a person/persons who weren't scared of attracting the wrong kind of attention.

Raiders.

We'd caught up with them at last. They must be resting up, before heading back to wherever home was tomorrow. We needed a scout. Someone who could sneak up close and see how many we were dealing with. Reports from the Fort put their number at anything between ten and fifty so we had to narrow it down. Jack volunteered and I couldn't stop this laugh that bubbled up inside of me and, as it couldn't get out of my closed mouth, sort of snorted out my nose instead. The idea of Jack – massive, heavy Jack – sneaking up on anyone, nimbly leaping over flora and fauna was just too hilarious an image. Jack turned to look at me and I expected anger or something but he actually joined in laughing.

'Yeah, guess not.' Maybe our friendship isn't over. Maybe it's the start of a new chapter.

Megan went in the end. She's light, agile, good at this sort of stuff. She wouldn't freeze in fear or snap a twig and go, 'Aaggghhh!' like a malc like me.

She was back quickly. Night ninja. There were nineteen of them. Megan's eyes shone. Nineteen of them. Fifteen of us. Her excitement was a living pulse.

'So we attack them now?' Raf asked.

'But then how do we find their base?' Lee joined in.

'We leave one to lead us to it,' from Megan.

'Leave one? You mean we *kill* all the others?' I couldn't quite get my head round us matter-of-factly talking about killing eighteen people.

'Kill, injure,' it's the same thing. Break someone's leg out here, you've as good as killed them anyway. It'll just take them longer to die.

'But can't we just overpower them or take them prisoner or something?'

Megan laughed in my face. 'Look around you – do you see any prisons here? Life here is survival. No one's going to shelter and feed someone who might stab them in the back.'

Jack interrupted, I think more to save me from Megan's tongue than anything, 'But, we don't know how many Raiders there'll be back at camp. Even if we get led there, how to we overpower them? We need it to be a surprise. Do we wait till dark or something?'

A hungry wolf grin spread over Raf's face. 'We wear their clothes and approach at first light. They'll think we're the returning Raiders.'

'Like the Trojan horse!' Jack's excitement conveyed his

approval. He'd loved Year 4 Greek myths. He was big even then and one month we played Hercules in People's Park *every* Sunday. I had to be Pegasus. Not so cool. I could see Raf was about to point out that, no, it wasn't exactly like the Trojan horse, but I dug my finger into his ribs until he squealed and didn't ruin this never-before-seen male bonding experience.

It's hard to smear mud onto your face so that it covers as much skin as possible but doesn't accidentally go into your mouth. It's also difficult while tasting a mouthful of mud to remember that this is the least of your problems as you're about to head out and try to kill someone.

We didn't light torches obviously. This was a surprise attack. What we did was creep. In groups of four – four, four, four and three to be exact. One group to approach from each compass point so that we'd have the Raiders surrounded. I was with Raf, Lee and a girl called Lara. She looked tough. She wasn't big or anything, it was just something about her face – the set of her jaw, the lack of light in her eyes. Our group was approaching from the east so had to sneak round the outside, wait in position and then prepare to charge. Lara went first and stopped at our post – a tree where the trunk forked in three. We could see the glow of the fire less than ten metres away and could make out shadowy silhouettes of the Raiders through the criss-cross of branches. Lee was bringing up the rear and at one point pushed through a low hanging branch that then swung back and bounced up and down sending twigs clattering. There was a noise from the fire and my heart went into crazy levels of palpitations. I tried to calm my mind, dull it with my new mantra: wait, approach, arm, wrap, neck, squeeze.

'Damn squirrels,' came a low, muffled voice. No one moved from the fire. No one came to investigate. I kept the mantra going.

We were waiting for Megan's signal. An owl's hoot. I've always wanted to be able to do an owl's hoot. I can barely whistle.

Focus.

In the dim light I could make out the glint of metal from Lara's knife. I'd wanted to take my slingshot but Megan had overruled me. Slingshots are for open land. You need distance between you and the target. These were the woods. This was close combat.

Silence.

Crackle of twig.

Hoot.

Then we were running, stumbling out of the trees and towards the fire.

Lara didn't hesitate for even a second. In a few bounds

she was there, straddling some barely awake Raider, knife raised. Then the knife was plunging again and again and there was a terrible life-being-torn-from-someone cry. So much for silent attack.

All around me were dark shapes of people running, arms flailing and knives stabbing.

And I couldn't move. I knew I should be helping, but I couldn't. I was frozen. I was useless.

I could count twelve Raiders dead. Most of them hadn't even woken properly. Been woken by metal slicing their neck. That left eight Raiders still alive. Megan was wrapped around a huge Raider, her arm forced up under his neck, choking him. His eyes were bulging and rolling in their sockets. His lips were blue and the veins in his neck were wriggling snakes. Lee and Raf were also mid-choke and Jack was punching some girl Raider repeatedly in the face, a totally freaked-out look stamped on his face. I almost expected him to start apologising between punches. Lara, Jono and Dan were stabbing. The others, I couldn't see.

Then silhouetted against the firelight, this Raider started to move towards me. He'd spotted me. I couldn't freeze anymore. He approached, but it wasn't a run, it was like a saunter. That's it, he sauntered towards me, and as he approached, his features came into focus.

His huge size.

His smile.

His melted face.

The psycho. He recognised me. He definitely recognised me. He gave a little laugh and started to sing to himself, 'Girls and boys come out to play...'

Then he stopped about four metres from me. Stopped dead still and smiled.

I needed him to run at me. I didn't know how to do the wrap round manoeuvre if he didn't run at me.

'I was hoping we'd bump into each other again.' His voice was gravelly, his smile that of a shark. He seemed genuinely pleased. 'You might want to start screaming now. All the girls start screaming some time or other. Particularly the pretty ones.'

I panicked. I ran at him, trying to swing myself round his body but he pushed me away so it was like all I achieved was a failed hi five. I fell to the ground awkwardly and suddenly everything *hurt*. My shoulder, my arm, my face. The first time I'd ever had to do anything and I'd fallen at the first hurdle. How the hell could I fight someone twice the size of me? I lay there trying to work out a plan – anything that might give me a *chance*. Then I remembered the knife in my belt.

I could hear his footsteps approaching. This time he was whistling.

Pretending to clutch my (genuinely) stinging ribs, I worked my left hand around to where the knife was – shielding what I was doing with my body. I gripped the handle and drew the blade out of its sheath. If I could just time it right maybe I could surprise him. A harmless-looking insect with a deadly sting.

I could hear his breathing. He was there, standing above me. My grip on the knife tightened, and I lunged up at him as fast as I could, the knife between both hands, trying to give my thrust all the power I could.

But I was too slow. In a blur, the psycho had me by the wrists, my knife pointing up between my trapped hands like a wise man's gift. He smiled that shark smile at me again.

I felt a surge of pain down my arms and he began to twist them round so the knife was pointing back at me. At my chest. He was going to make me stab myself. It wasn't enough for this sicko to kill me. He wanted to make me do it myself.

A scream tore out of me.

'Come on, you can do better than that! I want a proper scream.'

I saw the knife coming towards me, the smile on his lips, and then images of Cara, of Lotte flashed through my brain. I'd like to say I saw red but I didn't, I saw his horrific melted face and knew I wanted to obliterate it.

I wrenched my hands apart – the knife dropped to the floor and then the next thing I knew I was burrowing my thumbs deep into his eyes. Trying to burrow through the windows into his dark soul. It was his turn to scream.

But my hero moment was cut short by the full force of his fist. Ramming into my face like a steam train. Everything went blurry. I struggled to stay conscious, my vision doubling. There were two of him standing over me. He wasn't smiling anymore.

'Fun and games are over you little b…'

And then he stopped. Dead. He fell to the ground, and there, in his place, was Jack. A bloodied stone in his hand. I'd come here to save him, and once again he'd saved me. Malc Noa – the victim – the damsel in distress.

But the psycho was still alive. He was writhing on the floor, moaning incomprehensibly, and before I knew it I was on him – kicking him in the back, in the head, desperately trying to stop him doing whatever it was he did again. One moment, the knife was on the floor next to me, and then it was in my hand, raised above the psycho's chest, aiming right over his heart. I wasn't going to be a victim anymore.

'NOoooooo!!!!' Megan was running over screaming and jumped at me, knocking the knife from my hand. I struggled against her vice-like grip but she kept me pinned down.

'You can't kill him … he's the last one.'

On paper it would have been a terrific success. We were victorious. Lotte was still alive – Megan had found her crouched behind a tree some hundred metres away, her eyes screwed shut and her hands over her ears. Trying to block it all out.

Eighteen Raiders were dead to only three of our own. Of our elite team Jack had a bad cut to his arm. Raf had two black eyes. Lee had a swollen, messed-up hand and Megan had a deep gash in her leg. Save for some massive bruises, I was unharmed, my intactness a badge of shame.

There were no celebrations however. 'Only' isn't a concept with any meaning when people you know die. People who were talking and breathing and LIVING just an hour earlier. Jono, Lucie and Milo. I didn't know them really. I'd seen them around at The Fort and we'd exchanged a few words on the march over, but that was about it. Jono had shared his water bottle with me at one stop so I didn't need to get mine out of my bag and Lucie had the dirtiest laugh. As for Milo, I couldn't think of a single thing I knew about Milo and that massively bugged me. He'd died and I couldn't even really remember him.

Worse still, looking at them lying there, splayed on the

ground, my overriding thoughts were 'that could have been me' and 'that could have been Raf or Jack'.

Lotte wasn't speaking. The trauma had muted her. Temporarily we hoped but who knows. And every dead Raider meant someone had had to kill them, take their life and have them haunt their eyes. Neither Jack nor Raf's knives were bloodied. They hadn't brought themselves to use them. But that meant they'd killed with their hands, which was probably even worse. Raf looked shell-shocked and I hugged him tight, kissing him roughly, trying to take away his horror. He gently nudged me away.

'Not now, Noa.' And then he mumbled something about their eyes and lights going out.

The last Raider, the psycho, was under guard, his arms and legs tightly bound with belts taken from the dead Raiders. Megan had gagged him too with a strip of torn shirt. To stop his taunts. To silence his laughter.

We could have gone back then. Or rather forward – on to the Fence. We'd accomplished our mission, we'd rescued Lotte. So why didn't it feel enough?

After we'd eaten and wounds had been washed and treated with iodine, Lee coaxed the Raiders' fire back to life and Megan called a meeting. She presented the options fairly, this time there was no theatrics or attempts at persuasion – it was a free vote.

Option one: our 'elite team' pressed on to the Fence while everyone else returned to The Fort. The advantage being that we got to the Territory more quickly, no more lives would be lost in the short term and we could begin our assault on our principal enemy.

Option two: we finished what we'd started. We seek out the Raiders' headquarters and we destroy them like the cancer that they are so that they can never attack again. Never prey on the weak again.

Option two carried it unanimously. We were going to take them out.

No one was in a state to go anywhere immediately, so we rested in shifts, backs to the dead. I was on shift with Megan, probably because she didn't trust me not to try and kill the psycho. I don't blame her. I didn't trust me either. I tried to apologise for my uselessness earlier, but she told me to be quiet. I thought it was because I might wake Lotte who was a sleeping foetal bundle at Megan's feet. That, or she was too disgusted at my cowardice to even speak to me. But it wasn't either.

Megan shunted over, closer to me and wrapped her left arm round me, wincing from her cut as she did so. Up close I could see a film of sweat on her face. It came as a shock to see how much the battle had drained her.

Megan lowered her voice and softened it at the same time.

'Just try to concentrate on the task on hand.' There was a long pause and I thought that would be it, the limit of our conversation, when she spoke again, this time contemplatively. Almost as much to herself as to me.

'Killing people shouldn't be easy. It might be necessary. But it shouldn't ever be easy. It's the ones who find it easy you have to worry about.'

Then she told me all about how she and her brother, Simon, had come to join the Opposition. How it was after they'd seen her mum, a writer, dragged away in the middle of night for writing the wrong sort of book. She'd never been returned. And how hard Megan had found it to start with – the hiding, the fighting … the killing.

'You get tougher. It's like you develop a kind of armour that lets you get through it.' Her face grew thoughtful. 'But if you wear the armour too much, it's really hard to take it off again, to be soft again.' With that she glanced over at Jack, who was sleeping fitfully nearby.

'He loves you, you know,' I said following her gaze. And with that the armour slipped slightly, and her face lit up before clouding over again.

'You're strong, Noa. Stronger than you think. If I need to go away, look after them for me, OK. Jack and Lotte.'

I edged away from her. How could she even think about it? We needed her to lead our team. It would kill Jack if she abandoned us. Had that been her plan all along, get us to rescue Lotte and destroy the Raiders then send us off to the Fence alone while she returned to the Fort to drill her army? Just when I thought she could be trusted. Was one of the good guys.

When it was my turn to rest, I couldn't sleep. Couldn't stop thinking about the psycho and what he'd done and might still do. Couldn't block out the faces of the men and women behind me with their eyes permanently closed. Couldn't stop thinking about whatever Megan was planning and how she was going to break Jack's heart.

When Raf had suggested disguising ourselves in the Raiders' clothes, it'd sounded fun, exciting. Like we were all going to embark on a kind of mad fancy dress adventure. Turns out stripping clothes from dead and bloodied bodies isn't a laugh a minute. During the six or so hours that we'd rested, rigor mortis had kicked in and the bodies had frozen into position. We had to edge the clothes down and over stiffened limbs. Human mannequins where the joints don't work. The eyes were the worst. I'd imagined them closed but that was wrong. That only happens if you brush the eyelids down at time of death. No one had done that so the eyes were frozen open and stared emptily at the dawn. It's horrible how empty a dead body looks. The difference between a bare flat and a home. And if you don't believe in God – that spark, that occupying energy, where has it gone?

Megan sent Lotte back to the Fort with Lara as protection. One of our best fighters gone. But there was no possibility of Lotte coming further – she needed rest, comfort, sleep. It was clearly tearing Megan apart, sending Lotte away, not being the one to protect her, but she also knew that our mission stood the best chance of success with her at the helm. For how long though? Would she give us any warning before she left?

We didn't have a spade or anything to bury our three dead. We placed them next to each other and covered them with a mound of twigs. There was no time to search for sea lavender or white stones to add to the mound. Instead we stood solemnly round the makeshift 'grave' and one by one swore, 'Your death will not be in vain.'

Well all of us, except Jack. I scanned the area. Where was he?

I asked Raf and Lee, but they had no idea. Hadn't spotted his absence. Just when I was starting to freak out a bit, he reappeared – with a stomp and a crash and a baa.

He was covered in sweat, grinning widely and had a sheep tucked under each arm. His grin seemed to massively clash with the surrounding solemn faces – an out-of-tune instrument in an orchestra. But there was something so compelling about it and something so truly ridiculous about the sight of Jack as a struggling shepherd that it broke through the tension and the grief and we were all infected by manic grins and at least some of the pent-up emotion was released.

'I thought if we're meant to be Raiders we'd need to have some spoils to show for it!'

He'd searched the woods for the stolen sheep and managed to tackle them, rugby-style to the ground.

Raf was positively open-mouthed and Jack saw and laughed.

'Admit it,' Jack joked. 'I'm a better hunter than you.'

Raf's mouth seemed to go into a spasm, and I was thinking, 'Oh No! Not another showdown,' when he actually burst out laughing.

'OK. OK. I admit it.'

God, maybe they're going to end up best mates. Or I was right before and they're secretly gay.

Megan kicked the last Raider from sitting to upright. Time to go.

'Take us to your base,' she ordered. He got to his feet and jerked his head. It was clear enough that he wanted us to remove his gag but that wasn't happening. Megan kicked him again. 'Let's go.'

And so off we set, the psycho flanked by four of us at all times, knives permanently drawn. I suppose he could have led us anywhere. Drawn us away from the Raiders' base to protect the rest of them. But part of me knew he wouldn't do that. I guess I sensed he'd revel in the thought of more fighting, more bloodshed. And I felt he wasn't a great one for loyalty. No honour among thieves and all that.

We were a gruesome-looking bunch. Old leather and canvas clothes smeared in a mixture of blood and mud. Mine drowned me. Raf looked at me and smiled. Not quite the wolf grin but a husky smile at least.

'Looking hot, Noa Blake.' And I laughed and the sensation felt strange and good at the same time.

Jack looked even more ridiculous – his clothes were far too small – that, and he was in amateur shepherd mode with these two massively woolly animals at his side.

We were out of the wood and heading towards the hill we'd seen in the distance before. Heading into the hornet's nest.

We approached from the east with the sun behind us. In poetry having the sun behind you tends to mean you're on the side of 'good', 'God' or what's 'right'. We weren't going in for symbolism. Having the sun behind you also means your enemy has to squint and can't make you out as clearly. Can't make out detailed faces. Just figures, clothes, a general outline.

That's what Raf had said anyway. And he's super-sharp

and it sounded right so we went with it. Once we drew nearer and the psycho had, through nods and hand gestures, double, triple-confirmed that we were approaching the right settlement – that's the route we took. Megan kept consulting her compass and it meant we had to wade through some deeper salt pools before we were up again on the right stretch of higher ground. The ground was generally pretty swampy, apart from two raised routes to the settlement – one from the east, the one we were taking, and one from the south-west. I guess that's one of the reasons the Raiders chose this hill – they could control access pretty easily and there'd be fewer random passers-by. That or they settled here and then found that the land was too wet for foraging or growing anything so they were forced to steal from others. That was Raf's suggestion but I don't buy it – don't want to buy it anyway. I can't accept that previously good people could do such evil things. That's not the sort of world I want to believe in.

In the distance we could make out the faint tolling of a bell.

'What's that?' Megan turned to the psycho.

He laugh-mumbled something back. Angrily she reached for her knife. I thought she was going to kill him then and there. Maybe he'd served his purpose. But she didn't. she roughly cut the gag from his mouth.

'That sound?' she repeated.

'A bell,' the psycho replied, looking like he was going to topple over at his own hilariousness.

Megan kicked him in the leg and held the knife closer.

'OK, OK … it's a warning bell, obviously. They've spotted us.'

Megan turned to face Raf. 'I thought you said they wouldn't be able to tell?'

'It's probably just a precaution.' Raf sounded more confident than he looked.

The psycho was off again. 'Eeny, meeny, miny, mo … which way shall we go?'

'Forward,' barked Megan and on we went.

My heart was pounding as we marched. The idea of surprising the remaining Raiders kind-of-Trojan-horse style made me feel pretty sick but the idea of straight attacking them made me want to crawl into a hole and hide. Again, we didn't know how many we would be dealing with. The leader I'd seen when they attacked the Peak hadn't been in the party we'd killed so presumably he'd be there. And he'd need others to guard their prisoners. So best guess, they'd split their force. Nineteen out to attack, a similar number back at base.

In what seemed like no time at all we were close enough to see the settlement's perimeter fence, see its tin shacks sprawled over the hill.

The bell stopped tolling.

Megan kicked the psycho again.

'Well?'

'We've passed,' the Psycho smiled. 'The lookout's "recognised" us.' His smile stretched into a grin that ripped his face apart. I'm sure he has more than the normal number of teeth. Like a shark. Or this little girl in my block … my parents' block … whose grown-up teeth grew in before her milk teeth fell out so she ended up having a freaky-looking double row of teeth. Horrific.

I looked at Megan. Wasn't now the time to kill him?

She read my mind. 'And have the lookout see? That might ruin our disguise, don't you think?'

I'm a denser.

'Go first!' Megan ordered the psycho, her knife pointed into his ribs. 'One wrong move or sound, my knife will be in your heart.'

'Sounds like a date,' he sniggered back.

Sounds were intensified – it must have been the adrenalin. My boots crushing the tufting grass, the wind in my ears, the sound of the fence being peeled open.

'Welco …wh!!' The sentry's last words, if you can call them that, before Megan choked him to death.

We were in.

There was no time to pause, to think, we had to press on. Megan took us up what seemed to be the main route through the settlement. Maybe we should have split up, maybe things would have gone down differently if we had, but I think she knew, at that moment, that on our own we were fragile – physically and mentally, it was only the group that gave us strength. We thought we'd be meeting Raiders individually as we walked. That we'd be able to pick them off one by one as they emerged from their shacks or went about doing whatever Raiders do when they're not out ravaging.

This was the case for the first three we met. First a huge guy who looked liked he'd missed out the last few stages of evolution stumbled out of a rusted door to the left. You could see the emotions register on his face. Smile – welcoming back his comrades; confusion – these aren't my comrades; blank – Lee's dagger stopping his heart. The next two were pretty much the same although they were more fully evolved. Megan killed the second and Jack the third. We had to wait for a few minutes after while he retched over and over as he re-hilted his knife. No one even asked me to help. I am useless. I can't do this.

All the time I had my hand gripped on my knife, my adrenaline now spiking so much that my right eyeball would occasionally shake. We were heading to the centre of the settlement. To its heart.

We came to another crossroads of sorts and Lee, now at the front, gave a sharp hand signal – halt. He scouted ahead to peer round the corner to the left. Seconds later he re-emerged.

'The left path opens out into a central square area. There's a meeting going on. A youngish guy, with long dreadlocked hair is alone at the front so he seems to be leading it.'

The Leader. Horrible flashbacks came of him at the Peak. Burning buildings, knife to Annie's throat.

'He didn't see me,' Lee continued. 'And the rest have their backs to us.' Big swallow. 'Megan?'

Megan nodded slowly. 'This is it.' We were assigned roles. Close combat fighters were going to fan out and attack first. Raf and I were on slingshot duty – we'd provide longer-range cover and pick off Raiders trying to escape. I dropped to the floor and filled my pockets with stones, bits of metal, anything I could use.

My breath was shallow gasps and I tried desperately to deepen it. To calm mind and body. To Zen in with my weapon. I visualised the air as a cool drink and tried to take deep gulps.

'What about him,' Jack asked pointing at the psycho.

Everyone turned to stare at him. He'd been so uncharacteristically quiet since we'd entered the settlement that we'd all forgotten he was even there. We should have killed him when we killed the other three.

Registering our surprise, and most likely our murderous intent too, the psycho smiled and pegged it off back down the path we'd come up. Jack made to follow him but Megan pulled him back.

'No. We keep going. We don't know how long this meeting will go on. This might be our only window. He's gone the other way. His arms are bound – how much damage can he do?'

After a re-brief of the plan we were ready, as ready as we were going to be.

Three chopping hand movements followed by a point. Megan's 'go' signal.

And then we were running. Round the corner, into the square. The Leader was the only one facing us so it was his bellow of rage and confusion that caused the others to all turn round. Too late. We were already on them. One Raider tried to escape to the right and I fired off a large grey piece of rubble to bring her down. Another was coming up behind Megan and I floored him too. It was scarily easy to hurt people from a distance. The Leader had pulled two cruel looking curved daggers from his belt – maybe these guys are never completely unarmed – and started swinging them around. He was jumped by Lee and two others and disappeared under a tangle of flailing limbs.

The situation had become too complex now for our slingshots to be of any more use. Everyone was so close together it was impossible to ensure that you were going to strike foe rather than friend. Teeth chattering, I pulled out my knife and stared at the fray, searching for an entry point. Then my mind started to tick. Something was wrong. Something was missing. What was it? Suddenly it dawned. The psycho wasn't here. Why hadn't he come back? Why would someone who got off on pain and killing avoid a scene like this? Maybe if it meant he got to deliver a bit of uninterrupted hurt all by himself.

The prisoners.

I ran to Raf, tugging at his sleeve. 'I think he's gone for the prisoners.'

I didn't need to explain who 'he' was, or justify myself, Raf just got it.

'Come on,' he hissed, pulling me towards one of the Raiders we'd brought down. She was bleeding heavily but still breathing.

'Where do you keep the prisoners?' Raf demanded. When she didn't respond immediately, he pressed down on her wound until she cried out.

'Where?'

'In the yellow building,' she gasped, 'Just up from the gate.'

I remembered it. We'd passed it on the way. The way the psycho had returned to. Everyone was caught up fighting, there was no one to check in with, to let know. We took an executive decision. We ran.

Being right isn't all it's cracked up to be.

The yellow building was unlocked, or rather the lock had been forced and now hung lifeless from its chain. We pushed our way inside. The building had no windows and it took a few seconds for our eyes to adjust to the dim light before we saw them. Huddling at the back, in the dark, was a group of young girls, chained and dirty with desperate eyes. In front of them, arms no longer bound, stood the psycho. His now free hands were being used to pin a young girl of no more than 14 to a wall, a fleshy, unwanted necklace. Our eyes adjusted some more and I realised I knew her. I recognised the white hair. The pale, heart-shaped face.

Cara.

'No!' A guttural sound. I didn't recognise my own voice as I sprang forward. Raf, trying to protect me, pushed me back and I fell as he rushed forward, knife drawn.

The psycho, turned to watch us, his eyes glittering with amusement. He let Cara drop to the ground, as Rex used to discard a stick he'd tired of. Raf approached, making tentative swipes with his knife but the psycho just seemed to be able to pat his arms away. A minor irritation. Then, as if wanting to end this tiny nuisance, the psycho put all his weight into a punch aimed at Raf's head. Blood spurted from Raf's nose like a volcanic eruption and then there was a crack as his skull made contact with the stones. His eyes rolled in his sockets and then closed, but all I could think about was the CRACK. It was like in the road safety advert. The one they used to play all the time before most people had to give up their cars. The one where the malc teenager is looking at his scribe instead of the traffic and is hit by a car in slow motion. The guy's head cracked as it hit the pavement. The teen in the advert died.

Breathe, breathe. Focus. This wasn't over.

The psycho calmly bent down to pick up the dropped knife. And then he walked over to Raf's unconscious form.

'Stop!' I yelled, my lungs cracking. 'Stop! Leave him. He's ... nothing. It's me you want. Come to me. I want you to come to me.'

The psycho looked over, distracted. But that wasn't enough – I needed him to move. Preferably to run. Otherwise it wouldn't work.

'Come to me. Now!' It was a command. It had weight. His legs started to move.

I forced my feet to stay glued to the floor. I had to stay there until he was in range. This time I couldn't afford to fail.

Ten metres became five metres became four became three. It's not easy to stay still when you've got a six-foot-tall, lip-licking freak charging at you. But I did – I had to trust that if I timed this just right, it could work. Another step, and I was on him.

I used the momentum of his approach to hook an arm round his chest and then swing myself round and onto his back. I drew up my left arm around his throat, hooking my hand into the bend of my right arm, just like we'd practised. Then I squeezed. His thick neck sandwiched between my skinny arms.

At first he treated it like I was some kind of joke. Mocking me and telling me what he was going to do to me when I stopped playing round. But I wasn't going to stop. Not as long as I was breathing. I continued to squeeze.

The first thing I noticed was his voice. He was trying to act like I was still just an inconvenience, but underneath his words I could sense something changing – his voice was cracking, straining for breath. He clawed at my arm, but he couldn't get his fingers behind it. I could feel his filthy nails digging into my skin, scratching off anything he could get a purchase on, but I continued to squeeze.

Seconds later, he was gasping and choking and writhing, trying to throw me, but I managed to stay in position. I could hear his splutters, his last few breaths before he'd be unconscious, then his hands abandoned my arm and he reached over his shoulder, clawing at my face. He caught my ear and there was a ripping sound by my lobe. A scream tore out of me and I nearly let go. Nearly, but I didn't. I adjusted my weight and kept on squeezing.

Seconds later, the fight was gone from him. I carried on squeezing until he finally keeled over, crushing my arms. Even then I wouldn't release my grip. He was never going to hurt anyone again. Only when his chest stopped rising did I finally let go.

'Raf?' I knelt beside him and spoke into his ear, trying not to think of the sound his skull had made hitting the floor, trying to block out words like, 'brain damage' and 'vegetable'. The truly unthinkable – the d-word – wasn't coming anywhere near me.

He didn't respond. His eyes remained shut – not even a flicker.

'Raf?' I tried again, my voice coaxing as if all he needed to wake up was a little bit of persuasion. His nose was a congealed mess of blood so I couldn't tell if he was breathing through it or not. I put my cheek just in front of his mouth and waited to see if I could feel any breath, however faint. Nothing. I felt irrational anger at not having a mirror on me. That's what you're supposed to do, right? Hold up a small mirror and see if it steams over as their breath condenses. Well who the hell carries a mirror with them! I adjusted my position and felt again, my cheek now almost brushing his lips. On the verge of giving up, there it was, this fragile movement of air.

Raf was alive.

A tidal wave of relief crashed over me. What now? I didn't want to move him as everyone knows that's supposed to be the worst thing ever if there's any chance of spinal injury or something. So I curled up next to him, whispering into his ear all the soppy things I'd find too cringeworthy to say if he was awake, and hoping all the time he'd just open his eyes and speak – even if it was just to take the piss out of me. I'd give anything, anything at all to see his beautifully mismatched eyes or glimpse a wolf smile right now.

Megan would know what to do. Or Lee. I had to find them. Then it came back to me. The fight. Oh God! In all the stress I'd managed to block out the whole super important fight against the evil Raiders thing. I had to return to them. Much as it killed me, Raf would have to wait a moment.

'I didn't mean to do it.' A quiet voice followed by a sob took me out of my head and back into the room.

Turning round, I saw the huddle of girls I'd forgotten about in my rush to be with Raf.

The girl at the front, the speaker was probably not much over ten, pale skin, white blonde hair.

'He said he'd hurt me if I didn't undo the belts. I ... I didn't want him to hurt me.'

'It wasn't your fault, Nell. No – look at me. In my eyes. This is not your fault.' An older girl this time. Blonde hair but straw blonde instead of white. So they hadn't just taken Cells. A voice of comfort and courage. A familiar voice. No, it couldn't be, could it?

'Ella?'

My mouth was an oval of shock. Good shock, no great shock that here before me was Ella, my amazingly lovely cousin that I never ever thought I'd see again. That combined with bad shock, horrific shock that Ella was a captive here, victim of stuff that I couldn't even imagine. That I never wanted to imagine.

'Ella!' I couldn't stop saying her name. As if the repetition itself would make my brain accept the truth of it.

'Noa?'

She turned to face me. Her face a crumbling chain of emotions. Shock – pleasure – then something else – shame. No! It cut my heart. There were so many emotions open to her – hate, fear, anger, upset – but shame, no, never shame.

'What…' I started to speak, I had so much to ask, that I wanted to say, but Ella cut me off.

'Where are the other Raiders? We need to get out of here before they come back.'

'They're busy. There's a fight. I'll explain all later but I need to get back to it.'

'We'll help,' there was steel creeping into Ella's voice. Anger replacing shame.

I took the knife from my belt. The leather cuffs at the end of the chains were tough but they finally gave way under the blade of my knife and eventually all the girls – eight Cells and three non-Cells, blondes like Ella – were free and nursing bruised wrists.

The younger ones stayed put, a cherubic host watching over Raf, but the older ones, Ella included, came with me to help fight. They had no weapons in the conventional sense but armed themselves with planks of wood and pieces of metal ripped from buildings on the way. And the fire that burned in their eyes, the heat of revenge, that was probably ammunition enough.

We burst into the square, one of the girls giving this scream, this horrible war cry that chilled my blood.

But it wasn't necessary. The weapons, the war cry, any of it. It was all over.

The square was strewn with bodies, the survivors a

standing group in the centre. I made out Jack, Lee, Amy and Pete and a huddled figure that looked like Megan.

I bounded over, eyes averted from the carnage. 'Jack! Lee! Oh thank God you're alright.'

Their eyes were a blaze of anger. They'd thought Raf and me had deserted them. Run off when it had got too much.

But I explained everything, pointing at the girls behind me as proof.

And then all my words and emotions started getting jumbled.

'I found Ella. Ella's here, Jack!' Laughing. 'You need to come and help Raf. He's unconscious and he won't wake up.' Crying. 'Megan, oh, Megan – I did the chokehold thing, perfectly, I did it.' Proud. I needed to get myself together. This was not a good time to have some sort of nervous breakdown.

Megan hadn't said a word the whole time. 'Megan?' I repeated, crouching down to her level. Her eyes were glazed and, her face was drenched in sweat and she was shaking.

I turned to Jack. 'What happened? Is she badly hurt?'

Jack shook his head and tried to speak but couldn't get the words out. Whatever it was, it wasn't good. Jack was hurting and it hurt me to see him suffering like this.

'She's been bitten,' Lee filled in the gaps. Oh my God! I spluttered. The barbarians. Wasn't it enough to cut and burn, they now have to bite too!

'No, *mosquitoes*,' Lee clarified. 'A few days ago. She didn't tell anyone, didn't want anyone to worry, but it looks like she's been infected, badly. She fought like a devil but the fever's just kicked in and she's burning up.'

'Oh, Megan,' I whispered, hugging her. She'd known last night by the fire. Known she was infected but didn't want anyone to know. She'd fought until the end and I'd doubted her. Thought she was the selfish one.

Her face was blank, eyes bloodshot.

'She's not recognising anyone,' Jack said, his voice unsteady.

And I wrapped my arms around him and tears ran down our faces.

We've temporarily moved into the Raiders' houses. We'd exhausted our supplies and needed a base with water and food while we looked after Raf and Megan. Nursed them back to health.

With Megan delirious, Jack standing vigil by her bedside and Raf unconscious, it was up to me and Lee to sort everything. It was also a good distraction. A mental shield.

First was disposal. The sprawl of dead bodies in the main square was already attracting flies. We chose a wooden building at the edge of the settlement. It was surrounded by iron shacks so pretty self-contained. We piled the bodies of the Raiders in there, the rescued girls helping, and then set it alight. The flames licked their way over the wooden structure before sending out a disturbing, sweet-smelling snow.

Our own we treated differently. Four dead: Laura, Brian, Willow and Kyle. Good, kind people, all of them, from the little I'd known. Fervent believers in the cause. Lee found a spade in one of the sheds and we dug deep graves to bury them, setting a pure white stone on top of each mound.

Then we all just sort of stood around, unsure of what to do next. How to mark their death in some way. In the settlements, the settlement leader would probably say a few words, but with Megan battling fever there was no one who felt sufficiently 'in charge'.

Lee asked if anyone wanted to say anything and to my surprise Raf took a step forward. He cleared his throat and then recited a poem called 'Remember'. He said he'd learnt it for his gran's funeral.

It was so sad and so beautiful and finished with these two lines: 'better by far you should forget and smile/ than you should remember and be sad'.

And then I felt guilty. It's a lovely poem to choose for your own funeral but for someone else's? Can you really just grant yourself permission to forget them?

The job completed, we were all exhausted. It seemed like forever since we'd eaten and my stomach was in danger of digesting itself so we made food our next priority.

It seems that Raiding is a pretty effective way of sourcing stuff. Lee found a lean-to filled with dried meat, desiccated seaweed and mosquito repellent. There was a sealed tub of pure water and tarp-bath purifiers for making more. I guess it was more practical for the Raiders to purify it themselves than to try and lug barrels of water away from other settlements. That wouldn't exactly make for a speedy get away.

Ella, managing to prise her shadow, Nell, off her for a few minutes, took me to a pen with five chickens for eggs and a cow for milk – aka the mother lode! I recognised the cow immediately – Brian from the Peak. It didn't seem to recognise me though and did a massive snort as I approached. Cows are pretty scary close up. They also stink. Ella was totally unafraid though. She spoke into Brian's ear as she stroked it and then took a nearby bucket, squatted beside it and began to milk.

My surprise must have been audible as Ella, without turning to look at me began to speak. It was the first time she'd said anything about her time here so maybe the lack of eye contact was intentional. Made it more like confession or therapy or something.

'We were allowed out of the … that place … twice a day. In the morning to work on the water purifiers. In the early afternoon to look after the animals and milk the cow. It was the only way to see the sky. I … everyone got good at milking.'

'How,' I paused, not sure of how to continue. 'How did you end up here, Els?'

There was a long silence and I stood there awkwardly, fearing I'd pushed too soon and pushed her away in the process. Then finally, Ella began to speak. She talked quietly and I couldn't make out some words as she kept chewing her thumb mid sentence. Gnawing it by the knuckle.

'We, Mum and me, after we … left yours, we headed towards the Arable lands. Remember that guy, the denser, the one who survived there for about a year? Well we figured if he could, we could. We didn't get that far though. We made it out of the First City. It wasn't easy. [Big pause, open mouth to give details, close mouth to swallow details, mouth a thin line.] No, it wasn't easy. We got as far as the Solar Fields. That's when they found us.'

'The police?'

'No. They looked more army or something. They found us sleeping.'

Ella started swallowing rapidly and her eyes were filling

189

with tears. I stood closer and touched her arm. She jerked away and continued.

'Mum hadn't wanted to stop there, said it was too close to this building, that something wasn't right. There were sounds. I thought they were just from the wind vibrating the solar panels or something. Mum wasn't so sure, but I convinced her. *Me*. I was just so tired, you see?'

Ella turned to face me, and I nodded my understanding. It seemed really important to her that I understand and somehow absolve her from the misplaced guilt that was gnawing at her insides.

'They took Mum away. One soldier or whatever, he stayed with me. The others took Mum. And ... I could hear her, Noa. I could hear her screams.' Ella was full on body shake sobbing now. 'Then, then it was over and they took me to a Holding Centre and I was shipped off to be a Fish. The Raiders, they picked me up before I'd even reached a settlement. It was the hair, (hollow laugh), they were on the way back from some raid and thought they'd got themselves a Cell.'

Ella stopped talking and her whole body sagged so I caught her in a bear hug, trying to squeeze away her pain.

I don't know how long we stood there holding each other, but eventually Ella straightened herself, bones turning from rubber to steel. She bent down to pick up the bucket of steaming milk and we walked back to the central square. The milk tasted warm, sweet and was dotted with clots of cream. Real cream. Like when we were little kids.

Raf came to within a few hours. Lee was there with me. His dad had been a paramedic and Lee had shadowed him in the holidays. It must have been against loads of regulations but Lee's mum had died when he was a baby and there was no one to leave him with. It became a strange childcare-apprenticeship solution. Lee had been going to become a doctor too. He'd always been good at computers – it was like he could speak to them or something – but they were just going to be a hobby. Medicine was going to be the job. 'Why didn't you?' I asked. 'Become a doctor that is. Why give it all up and hack your school server? Kind of a suicide mission?'

Lee explained that it was his time in the ambulance that had changed everything for him. At first the paramedics used to get called out all the time. They were saving lives. All sorts of lives. Then it started to change. Fewer and fewer things were covered by the Ministry. They went to fewer injured kids and more middle-aged men's heart attacks. The pivotal movement came when they were speeding past a woman sprawled on the pavement. It wasn't an authorised stop – no instruction had come through on the radio – but the woman was clearly bleeding out. Lee's dad patched her together and they took her to hospital. He was suspended without rations for two weeks. The woman's injuries were a result of her being 'chastised' for taking part in an Opposition rally. She wasn't approved for treatment. The hacking followed soon after. A kind of 'know your enemy' thing.

Lee agreed that moving Raf was a bad idea so instead I hovered over and by him, a wasp that wouldn't leave the jam jar. Then, joy-oh-joy, Raf went with no warning from unconscious to blinking to asking to be helped up. Lee told him to lie still and was asking him all these questions – what's your name? – tick, where are you? – tick, how old are you? – tick, who's she (pointing at me) – 'No idea.'

My heart juddered and my brain cracked – Lee had warned me about amnesia, that it's a common side effect of head injuries but all I could think was, 'He's forgotten me. He's forgotten us. I'm just a stranger to him'. But while I was spiralling into darkness I looked up and caught sight of a wolf grin. The first proper, hungry wolf sign I'd seen in days and I was torn between snogging him and beating him to a pulp.

'Not funny!' I managed, trying to stop my mouth from turning up at the corners. Failing. 'SO not funny!'

I raised my arm to mock hit Raf, but Lee caught my hand and reminded me that we were trying NOT to move him so I lowered it a bit sheepishly.

Lee bent down to inspect Raf's head, his skull. It was difficult to see clearly under Raf's now pretty longish hair, but after a tense few minutes Lee declared there was no sign of an open fracture, that's one where the skin has opened and there's a high chance of infection and no evidence of a depressed fracture which is when a bit of bone can poke backwards into the brain tissue. So many horrific things I never knew about. I wanted to dance around and let out a couple of whoop whoops but something in Lee's manner made me wait.

'So I'm OK, doc?' Raf smiled, trying to look all cool and not bothered but totally failing to erase the anxiety and relief competing for attention on his face.

He tried to raise himself – I could see the muscles flexing in his jaw from effort but nothing happened. A shadow flitted over Lee's face. And then, even more scarily, he went into properly professional mode. He spoke slowly and clearly – managing me, trying to prevent a possible freak out. Certain words jumped out at me as if spoken in bold or italics – *'probably just bruising … possible hairline skull fracture … tests … just to rule out … the patient … significant spinal injury.'*

What freaked me out most was the fact that he said 'the patient'. Not Raf. 'The patient', as if he was distancing himself from the person, reducing Raf to a case study in case … OK I can do it, say the word – in case of paralysis. Which out here would be death.

Lee went in search of something and returned with a thin, sharp stick. Nothing but the best medical equipment for Fish. Starting at Raf's neck, he methodically made his way down Raf's body, prodding every couple of centimetres, checking for signs of nervous response. Each time Lee asked, 'Can you feel this?' and I'd hold my breath, only releasing it when a 'Yes' came.

'Do you know what today is?' Raf was propped up against a bale of dried reeds as I fed him our dinner of dried meat of some description and seaweed. There wasn't really any need for me to feed him. I think that just fearing I'd lost him made me weirdly maternal towards him. And he said it was fine by him as it made him feel like a Roman Emperor. I was his little serving girl; we were just missing the togas and the grapes.

So, yes, Raf wasn't paralysed. Just severely bruised with slight concussion-causing vertigo – making it difficult for Raf to raise himself. Difficult, not impossible. I'd never before thought what a glorious word difficult could be! Difficult, *difficult*, DIFFICULT. Shout it from the roof tops!

Lee had made Raf a makeshift neck brace out of a dead Raider's shirt stuffed with dried reeds and secured in place with strips of leather and instructed him to rest for the next five days. The vertigo should go. There might be other complications – if there was a closed fracture there might be brain swell, or haemorrhage or blood clots could be developing on Raf's brain. The only way to see, Lee explained, would be to do a CT scan which obviously we didn't have access to. He sounded apologetic as he spoke, as if he was somehow failing Raf. As if he hadn't been truly heroic. It's a shame Lee won't get to be a doctor. He would have been ACE. And as for there being proper brain issues, looking at Raf's now grinning face and glinting eyes, my lay opinion is a big, fat, NO WAY!

'Today? Do you know what day it is?' Raf repeated. I'd been miles away. I shook my head. Today rang no bells. Our first day in the Raiders' settlement? The day I found out Raf wasn't paralysed? The day Jack sat in vigil while Megan continued to burn up? Lee had sent Ella out to look for willow trees – there's something in the bark that if you chew it helps bring down temperatures. Natural aspirin. She hadn't found any.

'It's the seventh of August.' I knew this was supposed to be significant but I was still drawing a denser blank.

'Our enrolment day at Greenhaven FES.'

The cogs finally started to turn and then spiral into a whirl of panic. This was it. There was no going back. We could have been unpacking in our new dorm rooms.

We could have been signing up for specialist subjects. We could have been beginning a new and easy life as society's elite. Well Raf would be the elite, I'd be the slightly sub-elite category B. But we weren't. We were on the wrong side of the Fence.

Raf started to laugh, slightly manically, and I joined in, mania and all.

Then one thought stopped the laughter.

'Do you think they've questioned my mum and dad yet?'

Guilt filled me as I thought of all the horrific things that could happen to them. Maybe there'd be a few days before it got serious. Maybe they'd think that me and Raf had snuck off somewhere to be alone together and lost track of time. But I can't kid myself. The time would come, even if not for a few days. They'd be questioned. We'd be labelled Opposition. The Ministry might think Mum and Dad were covering for me. Even if not, they'd be tainted. Dodgy genes and lax child rearing. Would they lose their jobs? Lose their rations? Be shipped here? Images of Aunty Vicki kept flashing in my head. Would they … not survive questioning?

I turned to face Raf, wanting to drown in his blue and green pools.

'Are we doing the right thing?'

His forehead was a series of paper creases. Because his dad's so horrific I keep forgetting that he might be worried about people at home too. That he's got a mum out there as well.

'I hope so, Noa. I really hope so.'

When Dad was trying to 'broaden my education' he made me reads lots of old poetry. Really ancient stuff. There was this one poem that's really stuck with me. It's narrated by these scary 'hollow men' and ends with a line about how the world ends not with a bang but a whimper. I didn't use to understand it really. It gave me chills and spider leg feelings on the back of my neck but I didn't buy that things could end like that, got out so quietly. Especially if we're talking about people. People with passion and fire in their blood.

Megan showed me otherwise. No one knows exactly when she passed. She was breathing and making the occasional noise last night when Jack fell asleep next to her. He'd set up a straw mattress next to hers and hadn't left her side since she'd fallen ill. Lee's warning about the increased risk of infection should any mosquitoes fly by had been ignored, quietly at first, angrily later. Lee, recognising a losing battle, backed down and just made sure Jack had a bottle of repellent and was using it. Jack bathed Megan with cold water, pressed food to her lips, fanned her with his shirt and talked to her, trying to coax her back from the brink. These utterances of hers, whimpers I guess, combined with sleep deprivation had been driving him semi crazy. He was looking for meaning, trying to communicate with his loved one, refusing to believe they might just be fever cries and nothing more. It was like watching someone try to crack a code that they think will end a war but they just can't do it. This morning she was dead. I was woken, we were all woken, by Jack's cry. It was a bellow of grief. A call to a higher power, if there is one, to come and explain itself. A call for her return.

There'd be no rushed funeral for Megan. Jack had gone slightly catatonic so Lee and me organised everything. A team was sent to collect white stones. Another to search for sea lavender and rosemary. Another fetched buckets and tools to dig. I managed to get Jack to engage enough to help choose her resting place. At first Lee was against her being laid to rest here, in the Raiders settlement. He looked at the ground as if it was tainted. But Jack was adamant.

'It's what she would have wanted. This was a centre of evil but she stopped that. She led us and we cleansed it. Defeated the evil. And that's what she did – she could be fiery, difficult,' (he looked at me) 'aggressive even, but she looked at evil head on and actually did something about it. She doesn't belong in some valley of flowers or by some little stream. We should bury her here, at the highest point. We should remember her right.'

So that's what we did. The mound of white stones rose three metres from the ground and the scent of the flowers and herbs filled the air. It was majestic, it was beautiful and it was proud. It was right.

I remember Mum saying that when she first moved me out of a cot and into a proper bed I didn't know I could get out. I would just sit up and bellow for help, totally oblivious to the fact that I was already free – I just needed to swing my legs down to the floor. Mum said I must have thought there were invisible bars or something but I don't think she was quite right. I think sometimes it's what's beyond the bars that keeps you from leaving. It's the price of freedom. Maybe that price is too high.

It's time to press on. With the Raiders destroyed I think we were all beginning to feel a bit 'mission accomplished', but really, our mission hasn't even begun. With a detour to destroy an obvious and close enemy you start to forget about the real problem – the system that dumps half of society in a malarial swamp. The poorest half. Starvation, disease – these were hardly unforeseeable results. Raiders too, if you come to think of it, were pretty inevitable.

When there's no order, some fight to create a society, to protect others, some turn predator. Some make, some take, I guess. And the Raiders took. I wonder how long it will be before someone takes their place? We have to change the system at its core. Make the Ministry's accepted approach unacceptable. We have to find the server, hack the uploads and start some sort of rebellion. We have to cross the Fence.

Raf's been declared 'fit to move'. His vertigo's practically gone – he gets weird feelings in his ears every now and then and a bit of dizziness if he gets up or sits down too quickly, but apart from that, he can cope. And there's no sign of anything more horrific going on inside his brain – no nose bleeds, sustained migraines, that sort of thing – although Lee, voice of doom/medical saviour, says it's impossible to tell at this stage. Thanks Lee!

Amy and Pete are heading back to the Fort. They'll fill Adnan in on everything and help him rebuild and train. Try to increase recruitment.

The one massive issue and the whole point of the cot bit, Ella doesn't want to come with us. I can't quite get my head round it. It'd taken a lot of convincing by me for Lee to agree to take her. Raf was on my side, and I know Jack would have been too if he could have dragged himself out of his stupor of grief, but Lee was firmly against it. He said the decision 'had to be unanimous' and we couldn't be 'swayed by sentiment'. He banged on about ours being this 'elite force' and Ella not having any skills to contribute. We had to be a small team, he said. We had to be able to cross distance quickly, cross the Fence itself and be able to conceal ourselves on the other side. The more people we had, the harder it would be. Ella would just slow us down, put the mission itself at risk. She would be welcomed at The Fort or could return to a settlement with the Cells. Cara would look after her. They'd take her in at the Peak. I'd said myself how kind Annie was. The mission, the reprogramming of the Ministry servers, that had to take precedence over everything else.

I went mental at him. How could he be missing the massively important distinction? We could leave the Cells behind because they didn't get ill. They weren't going to die of malaria. They had special blood cells or skin or whatever. Ella didn't. We couldn't just leave her in the same way.

'We're going to leave the two other non-Cell girls behind,' Lee said gently, trying to calm me.

'I know,' I yelled back, his tone and his logic having the opposite effect. 'But they're not my cousin!' And with that I stormed off, running to the edge of the settlement. I sat on the ground and threw stones at a wall. Watching them chip bits away.

Lee caught up with me a few minutes later. We didn't debate it. He just sat next to me and started throwing stones too. On his fourth throw, he said, 'OK.' And that was that.

I raced to tell Ella the 'good news'. That's when she dropped the bombshell. First Jack not wanting to be rescued, now Ella. I'm starting to feel less like a gallant, rescuing knight, and more like a bit of a weird stalker. At least Jack changed his mind. Ella's seems set.

I get it in a way. If, and this is a big 'if', we make it across the Fence alive, we'll be fugitives, always on the run, always looking over our shoulders. Ella's tried to hide in the Territory before. She was caught. Her mum was tortured and killed within earshot. If you're weighing that sort of existence against remaining in a settlement with some girls you've befriended – one, Nell, who clings to you like a limpet and sees you as a mother figure – maybe being hungry and probably getting malaria don't weigh in quite as heavily as they might normally.

We had a last supper of sorts. It was a warm night, warmer than normal even. Jack made this massively long 'table' in the main square by resting planks of wood on top of reed bales. OK, so a few shacks had been sacrificed in the process, but since there wouldn't be anyone living here soon, that didn't seem like a big deal. It was supposed to be a parting feast, so Raf and Lee killed three of the chickens. The girls would take the others and the cow with them. I couldn't face any more death so I volunteered for plucking duty instead, which was probably actually worse. It took ages and turned a feathered, quite beautiful bird into something kind of indecent. The chickens were roasted on spits and tasted ridiculously good. Hot, juicy, probably dangerously undercooked, it was far too dark to tell.

As we ate, Cara asked what our plans were. I thought they'd known, but how could they? They knew we were trying to cross the Fence. That was it. Her question seemed to hover in the air and all eyes turned to me, Raf, Jack and Lee. They were eyes full of hope. They wanted to believe life could be different. That we knew the secret to change. With Megan gone, Lee's sort of assumed control so he answered. He kind of skipped over the actually crossing the Fence part but talked more about hacking into the servers, changing the uploads, unfreaking the freakoids. He's not a natural speaker the way Megan is … was, but he must have enjoyed bathing in the girls' rapt attention as he became more eloquent as he went on. That is, until Cara asked her second question.

'Where are the servers?'

This was met with total silence. We didn't know. We couldn't answer. The big flaw in our plan had been laid wide open and you could feel the girls' attention, their belief evaporate. They no longer believed in Santa.

'We know some things,' Lee continued, desperate to salvage something, for us as much as anything, to fuel us forward. 'They must be in a remote location, or the Opposition would have discovered them. So…'

Raf took over. 'So we're basically talking about the Woods, well probably not the Woods as people can holiday there, but the Arable lands or the Solar Fields.'

Ella spoke, her voice quiet and flat. 'What sort of building are we talking?'

'It wouldn't have to be that big,' Lee answered. 'The most important thing is that it would be remote, heavily guarded and the electric fields would probably create some sort of energy or noise disturbance.'

'Like a hum?'

'Like a hum.'

Ella started to gnaw her hand and her left knee was slowly shaking, tapping a crazy beat on the floor.

'Ella?' No answer. 'Els?'

Ella slowly looked up from the floor and looked me directly in the eye.

'I think I know where the server is.'

Everyone was quiet as we packed up ready to leave, caught up in their own internal monologues. Lee distributed the remaining food stores and we all filled flasks of water, not knowing when we'd next reach a fresh source.

Amy and Pete were the first to leave and we wished each other luck with tight hugs. We told them to say hi to Adnan for us, and that we'd see them soon. On the other side. That phrasing left a spark of tension in the air. No one wanted to think of the other 'other side'.

The Cells left next, Cara taking the lead. Well, all the Cells other than Nell. She's coming with us. It was Ella's condition of joining us, showing us the way, and Nell, who'd begun to howl at the prospect of losing her idol, looked instantly happier.

Finally it was our turn. We'd had to wait for Jack who, head bowed at the top of the hill, was saying a last goodbye to Megan. Lee was all for hurrying him up, but I begged him not to. He didn't get to say a proper goodbye to Daisy. This time he deserved some space to do it right.

We donned backpacks, and were off, a rag-tag, supposedly elite team. At least we knew our target. The Solar Fields. They were north of the Arable lands so we consulted our compass and set off north-west. We were all weakened from the stress and the fighting and so we'd agreed not to push ourselves too much. However, before long, our strides were lengthening, fuelled by a sense of purpose. A mission. Our mission.

Ella caught me up and we walked in synchronised step. She locked arms with me and flashed a smile, the first smile that fully engaged her eyes too. They sparkled as she whispered in my ear, a trace of the old Ella bubbling through.

'So, I actually got to meet the famous Raf.'

'Yup. And….?'

Ella stayed silent but did a pretend deep-thinking face to wind me up.

'Come on, Ella. He's great, isn't he?'

'He's got weird eyes.'

I dug my finger in her ribs and we both cracked up.

Acknowledgements

Huge thanks again to my husband for his constant encouragement and support. Thanks to Nina Duckworth, Sarah Brodie, Sarah Reid and Sarah Cornick for their invaluable feedback on early drafts. Thanks to my agent, Rupert Heath. Thanks to Penny Thomas at Firefly for being a brilliant editor and to Megan Farr for being excellent at PR. Thanks to Isabelle, Bona, Oliver, Lucie, Caitlin and everyone else who helped select the wonderful cover. And finally thanks to my parents and to my Aunty Jill for sending the first book to more distant cousins than I even knew I had.